ALSO BY CAMILLE LAURENS

Index

Romance

Les Travaux d'Hercule

Phillipe

L'Avenir

Quelques-uns

Le Grain des mots

L'Amour, roman

In His Arms

In His Arms

a novel

Camille Laurens

TRANSLATED BY IAN MONK

RANDOM HOUSE

NEW YORK

This is a work of fiction. Names, characters, places, and incidents are
the products of the author's imagination or are used fictitiously.
Any resemblance to actual events, locales, or persons,
living or dead, is entirely coincidental.

LIBRARY OF CONGRESS CATALOGING-IN-PUBLICATION DATA

Laurens, Camille.
[Dans ces bras-là. English]
In his arms: a novel / Camille Laurens; translated by Ian Monk.
p. cm.
ISBN 0-375-50652-7
I. Monk, Ian. II. Title.
PQ2672.A78365D3613 2004
843'.914—dc22 2003061631

Printed in the United States of America on acid-free paper

Random House website address: www.atrandom.com

2 4 6 8 9 7 5 3 1

First U.S. Edition

Designed by Cassandra J. Pappas

I have pleasant hands
You know perfectly well that nowhere else than with
Me will you find
The strength that you need and that I am the man.

—PAUL CLAUDEL

In His Arms

HE WAS THE ONE. From the way my heart was pounding, I just knew that I couldn't be wrong. I realize that such sudden certainty hardly seems credible. But that's the way it was.

I STOOD UP, left my still-full glass on the table, paid, and followed him. He walked fast, as fast as I did. I liked the way he was dressed, his narrow hips, his beautiful shoulders. I didn't want to lose him. A couple of blocks farther on, he vanished through a doorway. By the time I got there and pushed the heavy door open, he'd already disappeared into one of the flats. But which one? Not a sound could be heard in the stairwell, and the elevator was still on the ground floor. How to find out?

I silently went upstairs. The steps were carpeted. It was a fancy three-story apartment building, with two doors on each landing. Most of them had brass nameplates, and some were quiet, while others emitted the sound of voices, or the ringing of a telephone. Worried that I would be discovered, motionlessly listening and staring on a doormat, I went back down again.

———

THE MAILBOXES DIDN'T TELL me much: some had names, some didn't. They were of that ancient sort that has a slit you can slip your hand into. Outside, the gleaming nameplates yielded more information as they sent back distorted reflections of my face, but without helping me in my quest. All of the occupants were practicing doctors of one kind or another, except one who was an attorney.

HOW TO DISCOVER which one he was? He could, of course, have been the lawyer. He certainly looked like one—that said, I'd only ever really met one lawyer, a few weeks previously, and he looked like an arms dealer—let's just say that he was an ideal image of a lawyer, the way a widow or orphan would instinctively describe one.

But he could just as easily have been a doctor. There were several possible candidates, and I examined them carefully. Suddenly, their names no longer seemed arbitrary, and became more like signs from which I tried to extract a meaning, as one does from a stranger's face.

By some mysterious correspondence between people and places, the names of the occupants of that turn-of-the-century building all sounded ancient, their first names outdated: Raymond Lecointre, Raoul Dulac, Paulette Mézières, Armand de Sade—no, wait a minute, I'd misread the last on the list. Not Armand, but Amand, Amand de Shade, pediatrician, diploma from the University Hospital of Paris. That's right, Amand, I'm not making this up, it really exists, it's in the dictionary of Christian names as the masculine form of Amandine, from the Latin *amandus*, or "chosen for love," the most famous Amand being a monk who set about converting Gaul circa 680, as I learned from the reference book that I consulted that very evening. "Chosen for love" could certainly be him, it fit perfectly. While coincidences may seem contrived in a novel, in real life they answer to a need that surprises none of us. Amand de Shade, it just had to be him, elected for love and picked out for me under the seal of the deepest secrecy, Amand de Shade, the shadow lover that I now had to turn into my prey, into light, into a sun.

I nevertheless conscientiously looked through the other names: there was Roger Bosc, a masseur/physiotherapist specializing in post-traumatic counseling and, also on the top floor, Abel Waits, a psychoanalyst specializing in marriage counseling—they both worked in the same field, in fact. I eliminated them because, given that I had arrived in the entrance hall just after him, I would have heard a key turn in a lock, or a door opening or closing, if he had gone all the way up to the third floor. So I stuck to my initial intuition (first floor, left door) and jotted down his phone number (my elder daughter had a cold she couldn't seem to shrug off).

At that moment, the door opened, releasing a whiff of camphor followed by an old lady, who stared at me suspiciously—whatever was I doing there? I looked down at my notepad—was this the concierge?—then watched her draw away, slipping along the pavement with that ease of movement that people have who always wear skates at home, as far as the corner of the avenue—would I end up as sluggish as her one day?—at which point I came equally slowly to the conclusion that he, too, might just be a client, a patient, and I stared down dumbly at my pad—whatever was I doing there?

I waited. I waited for him to come out, to reappear, I just couldn't leave. I was scared that everything would come crashing down, that from a distance things would no longer look the same, that this was all meaningless. I wanted to see him again, I wanted it to be true, for the shadow to take on flesh. As the street contained no cafés to wait in comfort, shop windows to wait with interest, or bus stops to wait with a reason, I waited in the form of a statue depicting my humble little self at the foot of that building, as though one of those nymphs, generally found shedding the tears of fountains in courtyards, had been shifted out onto the pavement . . . Someone else would have gone about it in a different way, by inspecting the waiting rooms, questioning the secretaries, pretending that there had been an emergency. But I just couldn't. I could neither give up nor take action, only wait—but isn't waiting for someone a way of being with him?

He didn't show up. Distraught and numb, I waited for nearly an hour. I needed him. Several people emerged, but not him. I therefore concluded that he wasn't a client, that he worked there, and that I'd know where to find him again. I finally left because it was almost four o'clock and I had an appointment with my editor. And if there's one person who detests arriving late, out of breath, your heart pounding and distress written all over your face, that person is me.

IT WOULD BE a book about men, about the love of men: as loved objects and loving subjects. They would be the book's object and subject. Men in general, all of them—those who are quite simply present, and all we can know about them is their gender, they're men and that's all there is to it—; and a few men in particular. It would be a book about a woman's men, all of them, from the first to the last—father, grandfather, son, brother, friend, lover, husband, boss, colleague . . . in the order, or lack of it, in which they first appear in her life, in the mysterious shifts of proximity and distance that would make them change in her eyes, as they left, returned, stayed, altered. The form of the book would thus be discontinuous, so that the turning of its pages would mimic this to-ing and fro-ing, the progressions and ruptures that splice and split her connections with them: the men would have their entrances and exits, as in the theater, some would have just one scene, others several, they'd have a greater or lesser importance, as in real life, and more or less space, as in our memories.

I wouldn't be the woman in the book. It would be a novel, and she would be a character who would be revealed only in terms of the men she met; her outline would crystallize, little by little, as on a slide whose image can be seen only when held up to the light. Her men would be her daylight, making her visible, and even perhaps creating her.

I can just hear what you're saying: but what about the other women? Her mother, sister, girlfriends . . . Don't they have just as much, if not more, importance in her life? Don't they count?

No, they don't. Not in this story. Or not very much. I shall lend my character a personality trait that I have (and that I inherited from my mother), which has meant that all my life I have been interested only in men.

That's how it is. You can call it a defect, if you want. A lack of interest, a mental shortcoming. Right from the word go, she has been drawn only by men, and nothing else. Not the countryside, not animals, not objects. Children, so long as she loves their father. Women, when they talk about men. All other topics bore her, are a waste of her time. She could visit the world's most beautiful sights, see pampas, deserts, museums, and churches, but all such excursions would seem pointless to her if there were no presence, no trace, even just a reflection, a mirage or a shadow, of a blue man, a gaucho, a Christ. Her geography is totally human. If left to herself, she would never walk a single mile to contemplate a sunset, a cliff, or the distant contours of Mont Blanc—she doesn't see any sense in it. It would make her feel dead. She felt half crazy after seeing Cukor's *Women*, which features women and only women, with one of them occasionally crying out and turning around toward a door: "Oh look! Here comes John!" (or Mark, or Philip), but without him ever moving into frame. Not a single male form, not even a voice—it was unbearable. But she also hates war films, stories of male-stuffed submarines, of manly friendship in which women are just photos in wallets and fond memories carried to the grave. For men must reciprocate the overpowering interest she has in them. She likes men who think about women. Wherever she goes, as soon as she arrives, she looks around to see if there are any men. It's a reflex, a habit, just as others listen to the weather forecast: a way of anticipating the immediate future, to know if it will rain or shine. To begin with, attraction isn't physical, or not necessarily so, even if it can subsequently become so. She has no particular type, no special fancy—fair, dark, tall, slim, rugged, fragile—of course, she does have her preferences, but they aren't fixed. At the beginning, the man counts less as a distinct individual than as a presence: a global reality from which the eye homes in on what the heart craves—the existence of men.

She doesn't approach them, or at least not as some might imagine she would. She doesn't make a beeline to get her hooks in them, grab them, chat them up. She looks at them. She fills herself with their images as a lake reflects the sky. To begin with, she keeps them at the right distance so that they can be reflected on. In this way, they remain for some time before her. She stares at them, observes them, contemplates them. She always sees them as though they were passengers sitting opposite her in one of those few trains that are still laid out in such a way; not next to her, facing in the same direction, but opposite, facing her as she sits writing her book. There they are. The opposite sex.

NOW, SOME MIGHT think that this character was also me, given that I will be doing the writing, since I'm the one who's scattering around these sheets of paper containing what I have to say about them. It's hard to escape from that completely. But the truth will be irrelevant. It won't be my father, my husband, or anybody: that much must be clearly grasped. It will be a sort of double imaginary construction, a reciprocal creation: I shall note down what I can see of them, and you will read what they make of me—what sort of woman I become while inventing this inventory of the men of my life. This cliché should be taken quite literally: the men of my life, or, to put it differently, the beating of my heart.

Perhaps this would be the most accurate way to define the project: it will be after a grand ball where, drifting from arm to arm, and despite the headiness of it all, I shall have kept my dance cards up-to-date, and you will be able to see, as the pages, dances, and names go by, the varying parade of my beaux, of course, with their own particular quirks and looks, but, more than anything else, sketched in by the very motion of this whirl, passing from one to the other, taken, deserted, taken again, embraced, her heart pounding, the blurred, spinning face of the dancer, as the belle of the ball.

"DANCE CARD." That could be the title.

IN IDEAL TERMS, that's what I wanted to tell my editor. But of course, I said nothing. All I could hope was to be able to write it. He was wearing a white, tie-less shirt and was tanned. He asked me how I was, if I was well, what films I'd seen recently, what I'd read. I reeled off a few titles, and one in particular that I'd loved, he asked me why, what I'd liked about the movie, I explained that it was a really good film, excellent in fact, and, as he was staring at me with great interest, I added that I had really enormously enjoyed it and that he should see it too, it was great. He said that he had seen it, but had preferred the previous one, that all the nods and winks to Hitchcock were a bit heavy-handed, that an overuse of the ellipse ruined part of the pleasure to be had from the black-and-white footage, which had in any case been done to death by all and sundry over the last ten years, and that Kadoshki had already said everything that could be said on the subject as long ago as 1965, and didn't I think so too? Maybe, I hadn't seen it, I said pouring more tea—the pot was empty, my cup too, but I drank on anyway, while splintering the sugar cube between my thumb and index

finger, of course he wasn't wrong about that, but all the same—
I kept the cup to my lips—all the same, it was highly watchable.
He asked me if I wanted more tea and I replied no, I didn't, that
wouldn't be necessary. Was I working, had I started something
new, would I like to discuss it with him? Yes, or rather, no, I . . .
The waiter wanted us to settle, my editor got out his wallet, I got
out my purse, no, really, it's my treat, oh all right, well thank you,
then.

LOGICALLY, THE BOOK should start with the father. There's always so much that can be said about the man who conceived you,
who began the whole story. But I was rather tempted by the idea of
letting the editor appear first, given that I wasn't writing the story
of my life, but a novel (for I knew that my own life goes on writing itself without any help from me, even if I were free to give it
the odd personal touch and dictate its rhythm, and thus avoid
dying on my feet). So, as soon as I was back home, after first making an appointment with the pediatrician, I set to work on my
dance card—first spin around the ballroom floor, a quick waltz.

The Editor

THE FIRST TIME he calls, it's a Sunday. Her watch says ten o'clock; his says noon. He's just read her novel, she's fast asleep, and the heat's so oppressive that she's completely nude. She hears the third or fourth ring, dashes downstairs, and answers.

He tells her straight off that he was sure that she was a woman, despite the first name, just sure of it.

He's calling to say that he's passionate. He's bold enough to do that. Is it because that's so much easier to say when it comes to a book? She doesn't know, she can't make up her mind. To make such a declaration, you have to find the right words: passionate.

This isn't a professional call, it's Sunday, and he isn't at work.

Passion has made him call. A sudden desire to tell her that he loves her words, her voice, what she has been so good as to send him, to communicate to him, he just loves it.

She has no idea what he looks like, just can't picture him. But he has a pleasant voice and he is a man. The editor's a man, of course, the contrary would be unthinkable. What would be the point of writing, what purpose would such an activity have, if it wasn't a man who received it, and thanked her for it?

He's calling from the other side of the sea, he suggests that they meet one day, in the summer, whenever she wants, he'll be expecting her.

She remains naked in the sunlight for some time, performing entrechats. It's so good to be loved.

THIS SCENE SOON takes on the aspect of a foundation myth in the legendary history that every life gradually becomes while it is being narrated. It becomes known as the call of summer.

The Father

THE FIRST TIME he takes her in his arms, the father is already a father, and he knows what it is. What is it? asks the mother, from behind the mask through which she can still gasp in a little air. It's a girl.

The first time he calls her name, he hesitates for a moment. His initial idea had been Jean, like him, and Pierre, like his father: Jean-Pierre. That stillborn notion now had to be washed away, and the body named.

He calls her Camille. The mother has a slight postpartum complication, but nothing serious. It's nothing serious, the midwife says.

The father lays Camille in her cot. He walks down the road. It's November 10. He's now a father twice over. The father of two daughters.

The elder one is called Claude.

A YEAR LATER, the father calls. It's a girl. He's got three daughters.

He calls from the far shore of a dream, from the distant edge of his desire. He doesn't go to see her, he knows what it is.

It's a girl who can't breathe properly, she's blue. She dies the next day, the father sees her dead.

They call her Pierrette. After Pierre, his father. The daughter of a father three times over.

Claude and Camille are at their grandparents'. The father comes to fetch them—Claude? Camille?—over they come. Camille wiggles her hands in the sunlight—daddy. It's so good to love.

—Do you have any children?

—No, I don't, says the father, I have two daughters.

AMAND DE SHADE was a lovely, kind man, with an excellent bedside manner, my daughter burst out laughing when he said that he was going to turn her into a hedgehog with his tiny sterile needles—he was a qualified acupuncturist, a wonderful fellow all around. Monsieur de Shade senior must have been in the Korean or Vietnam War and had preserved his future descendants from napalm, or at least such was the love story that I devised to replace the one that had abruptly vanished as, hunched in a chair in the corner of the room, I took in the reality of the situation: he was Asian, about five feet tall, weighing in at around ninety pounds, and his smile could in no way act as a substitute for the tall dark handsome stranger I'd seen the day before, and who, I now had to admit to myself, I was going to have to forget, as we do with most things, the fact that we breathe and that we have the sky over our heads. And yet, as I went out, beaten and sad, and glanced absent-mindedly up the staircase, where a door on the third floor was being unlocked by a tweed jacket I recognized, the impeccable cut of which I was now appreciating through the doorway, as I was being showed in to my first session of psychotherapy, which I had been forced into booking with Abel Waits, because he was the man.

THE WHOLE IDEA WAS probably crazy, but this was the opportunity to try a new challenge. I was set on seducing a man, but not by the normal approach of concealing everything from him—or at least obscuring the heart of the matter. But instead by telling him everything—or at least the heart of the matter—that essential part of each of us that, once it is revealed, means that we are or are not loveable. If I really tried, I suppose that I could have worked out a way to meet him outside his practice, by going through his acquaintances, friends, family, by mixing with the right crowd, so that one day I would find myself sitting next to him at dinner and asking him what he did for a living, and whether he wouldn't mind telling me a little about psychoanalysis, because I found it such a fascinating subject, the inner workings of the human soul, though it must be hard at times, too, don't you ever feel like having a change?

But cunning didn't appeal to me, and I lacked the patience that went with it. The fact that he was a psychoanalyst not only seemed like a good way to see him rapidly, by simply making an appointment, but also a chance to find out at last what love really is, what I expected from the love men had to offer, what I actually wanted. In reality, the arrow that stuck itself in my breast like a scream as soon as I saw him on that café terrace was a stroke of good luck, a sign from the heavens, that wound prying open the two edges of silence. That blow to my silent heart, my dumb body, had been delivered by a man who was there to listen. It seemed absurd to go about things the usual way. With him, I should proceed as never before.

I'm not claiming that I devised any particular strategy. If, as in a traditional course of therapy, I began by talking about my husband, my married life, as they say, then this is because I was scared that I might be found out and sent packing, that nothing would henceforth be possible. Subsequently, I wielded the traditional arms of jealousy, flirtation, and seduction. But not very much, in actual fact. Of course, I wanted him to think me beautiful and I fixed myself up before going to our appointments. But that wasn't my main objective: first and foremost, I wanted him to get to know me, to know who I was, and once he knew me, to love me. I wanted to find out if it was possible for someone to love me when I was not a mystery—in the naked light of my pain and misery. For a long time, my palm had been stretched out waiting for a mite, I had begged for love from anyone who would listen. I had now found someone to talk to. It was him.

LET'S BE PERFECTLY clear about this, I didn't fall in love with my analyst—I just couldn't have lived with such an absurd cliché after all the others I'd been through. No, I was smitten by a stranger who, by the strangest of coincidences, turned out to be an analyst. This isn't the same thing at all, even if I did see in the coincidence a slice of good fortune, a promise for the future—what people call a lucky break. This was even more to the point since I had just begun divorce proceedings and my new book. I thought that my words, which had for so long been reduced almost to nothing, would now emerge to help me with both projects. It was, of course, rather ironic that he specialized in marriage counseling given that, it goes without saying, I'd decided to keep my husband well away from the entire business. But, on the plus side, this did mean that I could go straight to the point, to love. Thus, Abel Waits was ideal, the ideal man, whichever way you looked at it. So, when he sat down opposite me, by a small gray velvet couch, elegantly crossed his long legs, and said: "I'm all ears," the feeling of certainty that I had experienced the previous week in the café, where I'd first seen him, came back even more forcefully, and it was just as if he'd said, in the banal and passionate, pragmatic and possessive senses of the expression, it was just as if he'd said, with the same loving sincerity and flirtatious cheek, while snatches of the song were drifting through my mind, it was just as if he'd said: "I'm your man."

From then on, and for several months, as time flooded past me, there were only two solid points for me to hold on to: my book and my appointments, the solitary writing of memories and the spoken word of the monologues when we met. There were now just two kinds of men: the ones I spoke about, whose stories I revived in myself, and the one I was speaking to, who I was hoping would be the continuation of my story, or would perhaps revive me. Yes, there were just two sorts of men left on earth: the others, and him.

Alone with Him

HOW CAN I put it? I hadn't planned on talking about it all so
quickly, of being here in front of you, I made an appointment on
the spur of the moment, actually, I didn't want anyone to know,
not my children, not my parents, anyway what business is it of
theirs?—*what's it to you, look at me when I'm talking to you and answer, what's your interest in all of this, do I interest you?* It was good
at the beginning, of course, the beginning was just great . . . I'm
going to trot out the usual clichés, things you hear every day, that
you know by heart, age-old banalities, tales that drag their heels in
books, magazines, songs, novels, newspapers. I'm a school librarian, I read everything, I never stop reading, except when I'm
writing, so you can just imagine how well I know how stupid it is,
how utterly typical and stupid. The husband, the lover, the ex, the
exes, the father, the boyfriend, the pal, I know every category,
everything that's ever been written on the subject, the various
styles, types, and typologies: men who are cautious, stay-at-home,
distant, shy, overbooked, wary, violent, tender, depressive, passionate, or unfaithful, I'm not the first woman, that much is sure,
and not the only one, and this repetition is unbearable enough in itself, that discourse, the burgeoning triviality of those words that
have already been pronounced a thousand times and heard a thou-

sand times: I love him, this man, this guy, my lover, I love him, I don't love him anymore, it's great with him, to begin with it was wonderful. You talk about books in just the same way, or people, or events, or trips abroad: a wonderful book, a wonderful father, wonderful holidays—it's meaningless now, has lost all the power it once had, when it meant that you were filled with wonder, a terrible awe, astonishment, gripped by a sense of the marvelous— and yet that's how it was; you can also say: I've had a wonderful life. That's why I'm here talking to you—*are you listening to me, are you still with me?*—isn't it always similar, always so terribly much the same, anxiety mingled with time, the fear of death, destruction, annihilation, is there anything else, in the end, apart from that fear which pulls me along: a terrifying attrition, a wonderful erosion?—*do you know, can you answer, is it your specialty, what sort of a man are you: a professional, an enthusiast, a dilettante, a Don Juan, an expert, a great lay, a model father, a slippered pantaloon, a go-getter, a swindler, a dickhead, a great guy, a wonderful man?*

I don't know, I really don't, I don't mind talking about it, mind you, trying words out in my mouth for once instead of on the blank page—I normally write, I write about men, a book about men, "and how's your book about men coming on?," but I ask you, what else is worth writing about, personally, I can't see anything, it's the only thing that interests me—oh! his first interest in me, the very first time, I can still remember it like it was yesterday, it was fifteen years back, I've been married for fifteen years, all of fifteen years now—ruins, ruins that allow us to sketch in their former architecture, a monument to love with only its traces left on the ground, nothing still standing, no relief, nothing but the remains of solid foundations in the earth—in the earth, down on the ground, ground down too perhaps, gone to earth—but yes, at the beginning, yes—do I have to say it, is there any point?—in the beginning it was great, when we first met, it was wonderful.

The Husband

SHE HAS KNOWN him for barely a minute, when they go over to each other and touch—he says "hello" or something, a friend has introduced them at a party one Saturday night in Paris. They remain still and silent for a few seconds, smiling, then she thrusts out her arms toward him, wrapping them around his neck, and she closes her eyes; he receives her body, warm beneath his hands, he is hers.

THEY FIRST SPEAK a few hours later in one of the bedrooms in the flat, where neither of them has ever been before, and say their names.

It's the name she now bears.

SO FAR AS she is concerned, this kind of encounter attains utter perfection. With no words, they avoid the interference of lies. Love is when you say nothing—what could you say of any interest?

WHEN HE COMES, long after her, he shrieks like a wild beast (luckily the party is in full swing), he cries out as if he were dying. He has not asked her if she is on the pill, or anything. This moment includes the past and the future, it is an indivisible lot, take it or leave it.

THE MARRIAGE IS announced a week later. They get married before two witnesses in an empty registry office. Their parents have not been informed.

ONE MONTH LATER, she phones her father and slips into the conversation the fact that she has gotten married. "Who against?" he asks.

AGAINST HIM, sure enough. Right against him.

Alone with Him

WHY WAS IT so good in the beginning? Because we made do without words, because we got by perfectly without saying any of the things that are usually said at such times. When you have desire, words are excess baggage. Speaking, in fact, eliminates desire—no words can express it, certainly not those everyday words that just garble it, conceal it, pacify it, or destroy it. Articulate language is no way to espouse desire—I'm talking about spoken, winged words—only poetry can mold itself to your body. Poems are like voices, or skin. But the rest of it just can't. It's all a matter of base manipulation, or underhand trickery. Have you ever looked on in pity at a scene like this in a restaurant: a couple at a nearby table, a couple in the process of being formed? "What will you have? You look lovely in that dress. Have you read the latest Modiano? I wouldn't be bragging if I said that, in my group, I really am a cut above the rest. Have you ever been to the Seychelles? It's divine there. This Sancerre is corked. Could I see the manager please?"

There is something particularly obscene about showing yourself in public when still in the first throes of desire, about summoning the waiter, reading the menu, tasting the wine, talking about yourself, talking at all in fact. About revealing yourself, revealing to the other what you are like. How deceptive can you get? How can you possibly reveal yourself except when naked? In the seventeenth century, they had an expression for such seductive chatter, such chatting up, instead of "paying court" they called it "making love." "You will make love in the father's presence," to quote Racine. That says it all about the true nature of such flirtation, that chin-wagging designed to replace the body, or else lead to its subsequent acceptance, that mishmash of compliments and crassness, that tissue of twaddle intended to *manufacture* love, to bring it into verbal existence in conformity with the law, with society, as if love can be made any other way than by making it.

SUCH DISPLAYS of power are courtship in its most hollowly vain manifestation—I can seduce, I can shine, I can pay, I can . . . — I find that hard to put up with in men even if, occasionally, because of the powerlessness it in fact reveals, I have indeed answered with love, and have felt really moved—not by the suitor's words in themselves, but by the distress of a pretentious tongue concealing its timid flesh, those shaky hands, and the muffled tone of the voice. And whenever he got what he was after, it was always despite the means put to use.

LOVE ISN'T a social relationship. It can't be put into words, such things can't be expressed. Love can be translated only by silence or a cry, in the solitude of the flesh; it has never ever been subjected to laws. The father must be chased away from love.

YOU SAY nothing.

———

SOME MAY SAY: but marriage is social.

True, I did marry him. Did I in fact want to redeem the extraordinary freedom of our first encounter, our original sin, by dragging back the wildness of that untamed body-contact into the social fold, and clothe the nakedness of pure acceptance with a repentant "yes"? Did my Huguenot morality catch up with me? I am Protestant. My father is Protestant.

Maybe I did.

But maybe I also thought that you just couldn't let this sort of man drift back out to sea—exactly my type, the kind that takes you in his arms as a sailor embraces the horizon.

The Father

THE FATHER IS Protestant. This is something that she learns young and comprehends as an obvious part of her makeup: she is, too. She's like her father, she takes after him. His eyes are dark, hers are blue, he has brown hair, she's blond, but they are still alike. They're Protestants.

The father's been a Protestant for a long time, since the beginning. His father was as well, as were his grandfather, aunts, and uncles—his ancestors, too, Plymouth Brethren all of them, living around Alès in the south, all Men of the Good Book. Before marrying a Catholic, he made just one condition: his children would be Protestant.

The father is Protestant, you can see that right away. She, at least, can see it. There's something inside him protesting, some violence he has suffered and is screaming out. You can't hear it—it hardly says a word, in fact, it's mute. But it's visible.

What did they do to him? What happened? Where? When? The story has vanished, only the traces remain, the pain that molds his heart and shapes his brow, that dull resistance.

The father is Protestant. It's his way of being. She's like him, she sees things in the same way. They laugh, play, have fun (Protestants can be merry, too), but there is no reason to be happy.

At school, she tells everyone "I'm Protestant." Just don't anyone forget that. She's like her father. People may think that she accepts her place, that she's conforming, but not a bit of it: she accepts nothing—she'll never give way, never, not against the entire world. She is Protestant.

The father doesn't believe in God, or in the Only Begotten Son, or in anything else (he must have believed once, in the Father, the Son . . . but that was a long time ago). Perhaps he'd like to please his ancestors, those henpecked old men gathering in barns to wring a little comfort from the Good Book. But he can't, it's beyond him. Even when he sends his daughters to Sunday school, when he forces them to attend, he doesn't believe a word of it.

Nor does she.

She believes neither in ghosts nor in the Holy Ghost, and all she remembers from the Book is its literature: she protests, she's a Protestant.

Like him.

What binds them together is a God that doesn't exist, and a Revolution in which they will never participate. Their closest bond is that empty form; what creates them is that nonbelief in what they are.

Alone with Him

WHAT IS a man? Do you really want me to tell you? You really want me to try?

A voice, size, dimension, beard, moustache, Adam's apple, penis, testicles, testosterone, sperm, prostate, body hair, baldness, foreskin, glans, muscles, ejaculation, love handles.

Strength, bravery, sense of direction, reflexes, logical mind, straightforwardness, gallantry, activity, energy, authority.

Violence, aggression, vulgarity, cowardliness, weakness.

Alcohol, tobacco, gambling, sport, buddies, hunting, porno mags, odd jobs, cars, women.

Fireman, biker, surgeon, fighter pilot, baker, mechanic, docker, football player, champion cyclist.

Ape, primate, caveman, wild man of the woods, homo faber, homo sapiens.

Man of culture, man of good taste, man of honor, man of genius, man of wit, man of letters, man of confidence. Men of goodwill.

Man in the street, simple man, common-or-garden man.

Man of the world. Man's man.

Son of man.

———————

MAN OF GOD, man of straw, man of small means, nowhere man—a place between nowhere and everywhere.

Wanted man, hit man, man of good fortune, ladies' man.

Man and woman.

Man born of woman.

The Father

IT IS no easy task to find a photo of the father with a baby in his arms. Children smell of shit, they puke, they dribble, they sleep all the time. The father doesn't care much for digestive tracts—or rather, he finds it hard to feel close to them.

Love comes later, when the infant abandons its etymological origin and starts to speak. It then becomes interesting.

Thus, having a body is not enough to gain the father's love—it isn't enough just to have arms, legs, eyes, a round tummy asking for tickles and milk.

AT ABOUT the age of three, she hears the father talking to her, leaning over her and smiling, listen, listen, she can speak, she's answering, you can understand her, she speaks very well for her age.

You mustn't be infantile with the father.

The strangest thing is that he doesn't say much; all in all, he's rather taciturn. But she prattles on, recounting, inventing her world. So what if he says nothing, so long as he's listening to her?

She does the talking for him.

André

EVERY EVENING, at half past eight, she goes to bed. She sleeps in the same room as her sister.

Every evening, at half past eight, the father goes out. She can hear his metallic-gray Peugeot 404 start up in the street.

Every evening, at a quarter to nine, André arrives. He parks his Jaguar, his Porsche, his Cadillac, and here he is. He doesn't ring the doorbell—the children are asleep, and anyway their mother is watching at the window, she presses the button to open the door, up he bounds, here he is, he's arrived.

IN ALL THE NOVELS she later writes, the lover's name is André. She will not be able to change that name, or come up with a different one. The lover isn't fictional, he's real, with a name. The lover isn't a character, but a man, a real one. It's him and no one else. It's André.

ANDRÉ IS HANDSOME, elegant, and refined. He wears aftershave, double-breasted jackets, silk ties, bow ties, black or cream tuxedos, custom-made shoes, tailored shirts, and hats. He smokes Craven As in an ivory cigarette holder, he smells of Guerlain's *Habit Rouge,* his arms are laden with red roses, white carnations, rare orchids, he brings champagne, foie gras, caviar, he dances the tango, waltz, and bebop to perfection, he puts Sidney Bechet's *Petite Fleur* on the gramophone, she can hear their feet moving across the parquet floor in the living room, they're smooching to *Petite Fleur*—not too loud, the children are asleep.

Sometimes the phone rings in the darkness. It's for André— he's a gynecologist, he delivers women's babies night and day, people call him, he goes, he brings babies into the world, he rushes off, he leaps into his car, he's already miles away.

The father comes back around midnight, sometimes earlier, sometimes before André's gone. He sits down in the living room and listens to classical music on the radio. A little later, the bedroom door opens and the mother comes out, followed by André. The father and André shake hands, good evening Pierre, good evening André, they chat for a while, then André leaves. The mother showers before going to bed, the father carries on listening to the radio. At about two o'clock, he has a bite to eat in the kitchen, then he turns the lights out and goes to bed, too, without making a sound—the children are asleep.

SHE SEES the bouquets in the vases, the stubs in the ashtrays, some of the filters stained red. She sees the empty half-bottles, the crystal champagne glasses, the barely touched canapés. She can see the beer bottle her father opened—before he got an ulcer.

ANDRÉ GIVES HER beautiful hardcover books for her birthday, he says: "For you, my lovely." She gets her first "Pléiade"

French classic when she's thirteen—Guillaume Apollinaire—from him.

She finds him good-looking. Or rather, her mother does. Which comes down to the same thing.

ONCE A WEEK, she's allowed to watch TV until ten o'clock with her grandmother, who lives two floors up. She loves *Tonight at the Theater* broadcast live from the Marigny: you watch the old-age pensioners settling down in the hum of the theater before the traditional three knocks makes silence fall. At half past eight on the dot, the curtain opens. As the years go by, it opens to reveal the same smart yet sober living room, with its impeccably appointed protagonists—she in her shimmering tea gown, he in his dark suit, arms laden with red roses.

It's a love story that isn't plain sailing, but which generally ends up well.

When she comes home from her grandmother's, she says hello to André, who is sitting next to her rather sickly mother on the sofa, as though he's just dropped by to check her blood pressure, which he does occasionally with instruments from his bag, his stethoscope dangling from his powerful neck over his broad chest. She thinks how well André looks after her mother, and how lucky she is to have someone like him.

She goes to bed in a dream.

SETS BY ROGER HARTZ, costumes by Donald Cardwell.

Alone with Him

PHYSICALLY, what I like most about men are their shoulders, the line that runs from the neck to the joints of the arms, the arms, the chest, and the back. What I like most about a man is his stature, his build, his contour. Beautiful youths don't do much for me—unless, that is, they're already solidly constructed, capable of carrying the world on their shoulders if need be, or their partner in an acrobatic rock 'n' roll. I can linger for hours in front of Jupiter's torso, Apollo's bust, or Atlas's back. My ideal is like a Michelangelo study, or a Leonardo sketch, with the muscles of a Titan. I never miss sports on TV, with slow-motion shots of champion sprinters drawing air into their lungs like galloping horses, swimmers at the start of the one hundred meters freestyle . . . My kind of man is Zeus. I have a weakness for deities.

I REMEMBER—his name doesn't really matter—he was very thin, almost bony—"that runt" is what my husband called him—but he had lovely shoulders, at a right angle to the base of his neck, you see, and a very narrow waist, and when he was naked, you could just make out the skeleton beneath the athletic frame, but it was so beautiful!—you could see both strength and death. He had a magical expression for me, that opened my desire like a door, he used to say: "Come into my arms."

And then there was my grandfather, he was a famous rugby player, I have a plaster cast of him at home. He was a wing forward, both fast and powerful, it was wonderful to watch him running.

My husband is extremely handsome and athletic, he plays a lot of sports. I like men who struggle with their bodies against the fading away of the world, who slow down the advances of oblivion, I like it when men push themselves physically to their breaking point—then they come through, they're OK, they're still alive— actors, opera singers, great sportsmen, whose mad pursuits I find so moving, their agonizing ascents, their pain, violence, control, misery, I admire those bodies, those nerves as taut as ropes, their exploits, the records they try to break in the absurd loneliness of their sublime ambition: do what no man has done before—not to die, but to bear the weight of the world on their outstretched arms. To be deities.

To my mind, physical performance is not a metaphor for sexual potency, as some people think, but rather a depiction of man's triumphal despair, of the leap he must make to escape mortality.

The Singer

SHE'S HEAD OVER HEELS in love with him. He'd only have to whistle, and she'd come running, but there's no chance of that. She's never seen him, doesn't have a poster of him in her bedroom, doesn't know what he looks like, his face, his body, if he's good-looking—she's not even sure if he's still alive, from listening to him she feels sure he must be dead. Generally this is what she feels: he's dead and all he's left behind is his voice, which so vividly conjures up women and death. She listens to him for hours on end, as though spending all day making love.

He's Italian. Such foreignness is a prerequisite. It adds to her desire for him. He sings Verdi, the passage in *La Traviata* where Alfred makes his declaration of love to Violetta. In the already old recording she has, he sounds distant, as though at the rear of the stage, while the woman now occupies center stage forever. Thus, his voice comes from a distance, ever receding, as though he were being led away in the street, from the window, from the body he doesn't want to leave, but which he does leave, because he can no longer return to it. He has a fine, full, masculine voice, reaching us from the far side of the wall he is panting to break through, to cross over, to demolish—*misterioso misterioso altero*—and we go to the window, trembling we lean out and we spot him in the darkness, a gray shadow, a deep mystery, a shade, and we hesitate, we're frightened, he's singing, but far away, it's him, but far away—what is this manly voice that comes from a body and distances it at the same time, this voice conjuring up remoteness, the inability to be anywhere else but there, over there, apart. The man sings his absence, his voice makes a promise that it can't keep—his body. His breath and voice cover an infinite distance that can't be bridged, the desire they inspire will never be truly satisfied, and that void they bring us, the way they sing of the separation being gouged out here, in our bellies, makes us suffer the bitter pain of absence, forces us to feel the depth of the abyss and the extent of our failure.

A MAN'S DEEP VOICE, a man's voice pregnant with mystery, which splits forever from its master's body. A man's voice singing of desire and its gravity.

The Grandfather

THE GRANDFATHER ISN'T there very often. He's working in
his steel plant. He's at his rugby club, where he's the president.
He's playing cards at the bar of the Brasserie des Sports. He's
away traveling. He's in the hospital. He's dead. The grandfather is
often absent.

The grandfather is always there: on the wall of the study, in a
gilded frame, he perpetually scores the historic try that was in all
the papers that year, he runs faster than all the All Blacks put together, crowds leap up to follow his attack, and if you look carefully at the photo you can just make out Winston Churchill, mouth
wide open with astonishment, in the grandstand of the stadium
where these gods were in motion.

The grandfather is a hero. Anything else? She doesn't know,
but she's dying to find out. One day—she's thirteen and he's
dead—she gathers together everything she knows about him,
everything she witnessed and everything she's been told. There
isn't much: in material terms, you could fit it into a cookie jar.

1. One Thursday at a fair, he pays for some Gypsy children in
rags to go on the rides.

2. He teaches her to tell the time and together they make a cardboard clock, whose hands are fixed in place and moved by a cork. The face is blue, the color of time.

3. He knows where to go mushrooming, the habits of trout, and the names of trees.

4. He can draw better than anyone else, you just ask him to make a picture of whatever occurs to you and he gets it spot on.

5. He's an engineer. His father was an elementary-school teacher.

6. During the war, he was called in three times by the Gestapo because entire consignments of metal were vanishing into thin air.

7. He knows important people, he invites Monsieur Chaban-Delmas, another hero, to dinner.

8. He causes a lot of jealousy, even among his friends and his brothers.

9. He smokes, he smokes all the time, he's had four strokes. He has also had a stomach ulcer, and he almost lost an arm when his sleeve got caught in a machine at his factory.

10. The doctor warns him: "If you don't stop smoking, the next time you'll be a goner." But he's a man, he's strong, he isn't afraid to die.

11. He lays his hand on her head (she loves him, she loves him so much . . .), tweaks her nose, and tells her solemnly: "You're destined for great things."

12. She'll do whatever he wants her to do. She loves him.

The Great-Uncle

HE'S HER GRANDFATHER'S brother. Every summer, she sees him in the village in the Tarn where they were born and they now share the family house—one floor each—during the holidays.

Every summer, she arrives in triumph in her grandfather's Citroën. She's four, five, six, she'd go to the end of the world with him. He takes her fishing, berrying, and mushrooming. Every time they spot the church steeple around a bend in the road from the top of a meadow, he takes off his tweed cap and says portentously, so as to make her laugh: "Here, a great man was born." She laughs, but she also believes him. She believes that there is no stronger man in the world than her grandfather—not a single one.

One evening, he dies. She's nine years old, she recites poems to him that she has learned at school: *Demain dès l'aube à l'heure où blanchit la campagne, Ô buffet du vieux temps, tu sais bien des histoires Et tu voudrais conter tes contes, et bruis Quand s'ouvrent lentement tes grandes portes noires*, but nothing doing, he's smoked too much, too often, hiding in the bathroom, so he dies.

The next day, the whole family's there, some of them from far away, in a state of agitation. Everyone moans and cries, isn't it always like this, the best depart first? She forces herself to look merry, to cheer up her grandmother and her mother, she's too young, she wouldn't understand.

She goes down to the vegetable patch beside the main road to look at the lettuces her grandfather planted. The great-uncle is there, holding a spade. When she leans back against the little stone wall, he comes over to her. She smiles at him. He puts his hand on her back, then slips it inside her shorts to stroke her buttocks, undo the button, she doesn't have any hair yet but she soon will, and she likes that, doesn't she, all girls like that, and he likes it too, just look.

He does it again after the funeral, after the meal. She takes refuge with the neighboring farmers she's known ever since she was tiny. They're drinking coffee. The great-uncle follows her inside and they offer him a drop of brandy, so he sits down on the bench beside her then, while chatting and smoking, he puts his hand between her thighs and leaves it there. She's expecting them to say something, all of them, especially the farmer's wife or her daughters-in-law, she wants them to save her. But no one says a word, they stare at her, she doesn't dare move, she stays put as if everything were fine, the little slut.

ONE MORNING, she goes to see her grandmother and tells. The grandmother is sweeping the balcony, it's a lovely day, her face is drawn, pale with grief. As soon as she starts speaking, the grandmother shoves her inside into the bedroom with its yellow double bed. She takes her by the shoulders, crouches down, and says, straight into her face:

"Never repeat what you've just told me. Do you hear me? Never."

Alone with Him

DO I HAVE any girlfriends, women I'm close to? No. Not at all. I've never really trusted any, I don't know, I've never confided in a woman, not once.

Why?

Alone with Him

THE FOLLOWING WINTER, I had a huge furuncle on the top of my thigh, it was agony, and, so far as I remember, it was quite dangerous, it had to be pierced and the pus removed. My father did it: there I was sitting in my knickers, legs splayed, and my father with his face just above it, aiming a needle or something, and my mother holding my hand as though I was about to give birth—I say that because the whole scene suddenly came back to me when I was pregnant for the first time, I'd buried it, wiped it out, then it came back so clearly in the light of my tears, teeth clenched to stop myself from screaming, with this image: my father between my legs removing a malevolent seed.

That same year—a bad year full of sickness and injury—I twisted my ankle. This time, it was André who came to treat me, because he was a doctor. When he'd finished dressing it, he kissed me—he smelled of aftershave—and said: "It will soon be over, my lovely, you'll soon be rid of your twisted uncle."

—Yes.

—Yes, yes, indeed. Bodies speak with their own words, words are even part of the body, they leave it, then return, don't think I don't know that! Bodies are full to the gills with words, fur uncle, twisted ankle, it's obvious, but no one listens. Even you who are there to listen, you hear nothing, understand nothing, pretend everything's fine—but bodies really aren't that complicated, there aren't that many letters in the alphabet, words are scarce, bodies are simple, they're language made plain. In fact, everyone speaks it, but no one understands it. And here I am trailing around this body no one listens to. It'll be the death of me, I tell you, it really will be the death of me.

The Fantasy Man

SHE'S TAKEN INTO his presence and shoved toward him. Sitting upright, his features motionless, dark hair, he utters curt, guttural orders in a foreign language. An interpreter tells her to get undressed, she refuses, the man gestures, she cries out, they force her to.

She's naked in front of him. He makes her twirl around, stand with her back to him, bend over, he examines her breasts, weighs them, puts a finger in each orifice, measures her waist, her hips, opens her buttocks, takes down her hair, lifts it up, fingers it, tells her to lean over in an arch, to kneel down, lie flat, on all fours, for a gynecological examination, in prayer, he inspects her mouth, teeth, nipples, vulva, and nails.

THEY DYE her hair honey blond, change it from being straight into an avalanche of curls, which they puff up and reset every morning.

They inject a product containing collagen into her lips, fleshing them up and thickening them.

They give her implants, which increase her breasts by two sizes, and tattoo her nipples brown.

They depilate her pubis, armpits, and legs.

They file, polish, and varnish her nails.

They make her do bodybuilding exercises to firm up her buttocks—hundreds of them, for hours on end.

They teach her to obey orders given in a variety of languages, to walk in high heels, to smile, to offer herself—from behind, face on, to everyone's pleasure.

They give her daily training in fellatio, in sodomy, they build up her perineum muscles using dildos, they make her practice various positions, how to satisfy various tastes, how to be taken by several at the same time without disappointing anyone, how to respond to demands.

THREE MONTHS LATER, she's ready. With her varnished nails and wavy locks, she wears skintight panties, split at the front and the back, and a bra that almost completely reveals her heavy breasts. The man tries her out, passes her around, gets her tested and evaluated.

Then she's put out into circulation. She serves at table and in the smoking room, answers to bells, gestures, words, does everything the men want, keeps her panties on if they prefer, takes them off if they ask her to—some snip them in half with scissors.

When no one asks for her, she stands by the door, her breasts pressed in, butt sticking out, lips pouting, or else, beside an armchair, she acts as a side table, on which they place a large cold marble ashtray.

The Father

SO WHERE DOES the father go every evening at half past eight, while André is seeing her mother?

Where does he go? This burning but nevertheless quite straightforward question was to be answered shortly during a conversation at the swimming pool with André's children: every evening, at half past eight, the father goes to see André's wife.

THE FATHER IS an uncomplicated man. She doesn't know how it all started, how the crossover was effected, and she never dares ask. She just reckons that he wasn't the one who started—the father is certainly not one for intrigues and affairs—but, when he had to adapt to a new situation, he chose the simplest, though perhaps not the most satisfying, solution. He had to do something, and André's wife was, in every respect—in terms of pride, revenge, despair, or a liking for symmetry—the simplest way out.

The Father

THE FATHER HAS simple tastes. He listens to classical music, a few records he was presumably given long ago—he never buys any new ones. Occasionally, something on the radio appeals to him—a Georges Brassens song or an airy Pink Floyd melody—but he never tries to acquire it or listen to it again. He takes things as they come, he doesn't try to hasten them along, he has no desires, only tastes. Anything that requires conquest, application, or willpower, he does without.

The same goes for women.

On Sunday, he asks them to wake him up so he can listen to comedians like Pierre Dac or Francis Blanche on the radio, or sketches by Fernand Raynaud. He laughs till he cries, with her sitting on his lap, she doesn't get all the jokes—*Would you say "Fortitude and Luck" Reverend Spooner?—I think I'd better not*—he doesn't explain them to her, she'll understand in time. He also has some Jean Rigaud records in his wardrobe, which are forbidden to kids, and she plays them during the afternoon on the gramophone, which is also forbidden—*Ah! Me old mate!—The Skin of My Bollocks with It*—they're live performances and the crowd screams with laughter.

Then the father reads. The mother makes bulk purchases of

one-franc detective stories for him, which she then takes back and exchanges for others—sometimes he's read them already, which he realizes after five or six pages. On the cover, there's always a scantily clad girl wearing boots or a low-cut dress; she's either holding a revolver or else stands nonchalantly in the sights of a gun. As soon as she can, she reads them—San Antonio, SAS—they seem very similar to her, the story's always the same, with exciting passages in great detail, during which girls die after being raped, and with punning titles setting the scene in barbaric countries no one ever visits.

Sometimes the father goes to the movies. He sees the latest James Bond, in fact, everyone says he looks like Sean Connery. Or else a film by Arthur Rubinstein, along with his daughters who don't take music lessons, because they would make too much noise in the house.

The Father

THE FATHER HAS only a father, no mother. When they visit the family in the south, which they do infrequently because it's so far, she notices that there is no grandmother on her father's side. She has a grandfather, great-aunts and their husbands, plus some second cousins—but no grandmother.

And yet, the father isn't an orphan. There's no grave, no grief, no sorrow. She must once have existed, he must have met her at least once, but no one ever mentions her. There are no photos, no souvenirs, no memories. If any exist in the father's mind, no one is any the wiser, there is complete silence.

THE FATHER SOMETIMES has a sad or stern look on his face, tinged with slight resentment. Maybe he's wondering if his mother's forgotten him.

She often thinks about the father. She tries to imagine what his childhood must have been like. She has difficulty picturing him as a boy, how was that ever possible? She feels sorry for him.

———

ONE DAY, at dinner, the father announces: "Next Thursday, my mother's coming to have lunch with us." Then, seeing the amazed expressions on his daughters' faces, he adds in exasperation: "You know, your grandmother."

No, they don't.

He must have asked her to come on a Thursday on purpose: he works that day, it's even his busiest time of the week, but they're off school. Claude is fourteen, she is twelve. They think the father really should make an effort to explain what's going on. But he doesn't. The father has a mother. That's all there is to it.

No comment.

THE FATHER'S MOTHER arrives as arranged, just before noon. The father says: "Good morning, Madame." Lunch is served at once, because he has several appointments and must be back at his surgery by two. The father has other fish to fry.

His mother doesn't. In fact, she'd just love to pop into his office, to see how he's doing, how successful he is, as chance would have it, she has a toothache, so if he could take a look, if he could examine her, just briefly. Her granddaughters will show her the way, how about around four . . . her train is at seven-oh-two, meanwhile they'll go shopping, she means to buy presents for them all, she didn't have time before coming, and anyway she was worried she might not buy the right thing, she doesn't know what they like, she just doesn't, what's more, it's extremely awkward carrying parcels on the train, and she'd like to have some photos taken, to get portraits done by a photographer, she doesn't have any photos of them.

The father doesn't have any photos either. And not enough time to have any taken. And no desire to examine his mother. But if she really does have a toothache . . .

THE GRANDMOTHER BUYS them some records by the Bee Gees. They'd have preferred Johnny Hallyday's *Que je t'aime,* but they don't dare ask: the father has strictly forbidden it because it isn't a song that is suitable for girls their age.

AT FOUR O'CLOCK, the three of them are sitting in the waiting room. The grandmother asks them questions about what they'd like to do when they're grown up—they have no idea.

They go into the examination room. The father busies himself getting various instruments ready. His mother peers round and looks pleased, she also looks at him: handsome, tall, forty, all his own teeth—the last time, he had only eight of them. She feels proud in her maternal heart.

SHE LEFT FOR another man—a man other than her husband. Her husband explained to her clearly: if she went, she'd never see the baby again, she'd lose all her rights. He presented her with a choice: "your child or that fellow." She took the fellow.

So the father has a rival—a fortunate rival. This situation is both difficult and durable. It's been going on almost since he was born. The father is a born loser. He doesn't look it. You wouldn't believe it when you saw him.

HE ASKS his mother to sit down in the reclining chair: "Please, take a seat," he says.

The noise of the drill is unbearable. They sit in the corner and read the sleeve notes on their records. They're dying for it to be seven-oh-two.

The father fills out a health insurance claim. The grandmother opens her purse and takes out two bills. He gives her her change.

NOTHING IS KNOWN about the father, about his history, except this: he makes his mother pay.

Alone with Him

"MARRIAGE COUNSELING." Quite a concept, really, don't you think?

Do you imagine that marriages can be guided? Like missiles? "I'm married, but I'm being counseled," is that it?

I should have gone to see the lawyer downstairs.

Can you better a relationship, retie a loose knot? How?

It takes two, does it? Why? To guide each other out of couple-dom?

My husband would never agree to come—never, that much I'm sure of.

Besides, there's two of us already. You and me. That makes two.

OK, I'LL STOP fooling around. You don't like it when I have any fun.

What I meant is that there's no being counseled out of being a couple. Etymologically, "conjugal" means being yoked together, man and woman, like oxen yoked to the plow, but it's like trying to couple a mouse and a tiger, or rather, to avoid the size discrepancy, a mouse and a lizard—I'll leave you to guess which one's the lizard.

To sum up, I just don't see any relationship between them. You're pretending there is one, but you should be the first person to know that there just isn't.

The best you can hope for is a drawing together. The goal would be to draw me closer to the man. But not so close that I could grab him or unite with him. Just for one dance. A quick waltz, with light showing between the bodies. A mouse and a lizard caught for one instant in the same sunbeam.

Do you think a man and a woman dancing together constitutes a couple? A union likely to result in unity?

To my mind, it makes two—in a couple, there are two of you, that much is clear, and I just don't see any relationship between them.

HOW CAN YOU counsel dancers when the ball is over?

The Father

THE FATHER HAS SUFFERED a lot, that much is clear. He's a poor old daddy without a mommy.

She draws little, gaily colored pictures for him. She writes poems and nursery rhymes, which she can't leave under his pillow, because of André, so instead she slips them into the pocket of his pajamas, which hang on the hook in the bathroom. Every day, when she's finished her homework, she makes up a new refrain, more verses dedicated to her daddy, her papa, her *papounet*. As soon as she gets home from school, she puts on the leather slippers she gave him for his birthday, she's lost inside them, but it's a nice feeling, like she was with him, in a sort of tryst; she keeps up this slippery intimacy.

She's in her first year at grade school, one year ahead. At elementary school, she was always first or second in her class, and now every term she aims at getting honors, she wants to be the best. She's pretty, lively, sweet, polite, tender, well behaved, well brought up, attentive, sensitive, and loving. This way, the father will be proud of her and, when she clambers up onto his lap after lunch and dinner, he'll smile at her.

THUS, DURING the final months of her childhood, her ideal man takes shape, defined as follows: a man who has suffered, but who can be made happy. When she turns into a woman, the little girl will not become a man-eater. On the contrary, whenever she's attracted to a man, her greatest ambition, her dearest wish, especially if he's sad and miserable, will be to make him happy.

The Fiancé

HER CHILDHOOD IS crowded with fiancés. Unlike many girls, she can't recall a time when she disliked boys: they are all around her, as far back as she can remember, as though she were both the light and the shadow that defines them. It was probably the only time in her life when she exploited them—childhood is full of objects and toys you drop as soon as they break. But they also introduce her to the pain of love.

The first one has the same Christian name as the husband she will marry twenty years later. He lost one of his hands when a car caught fire. He's four, and when she dances with him at nursery school—always with him, she has no other partners—she guides him cautiously through the throng by his elbow. She's sad when he moves to a nearby village and the next time she sees him is ten years later in a newspaper photograph, which shows him climbing a sheer rock face with his one bare hand.

The second one is called Lionel. When she arrives in misery at summer camp, where she is to spend one month away from her mother, he tells her that he's there for two, and it's the same every year: he's an orphan, brought up by the Social Services—she doesn't understand what that means. When she appears as the fairy in the show put on by the seven- and eight-year-olds—he's eleven—he gives her a standing ovation and asks for a kiss, which she grants him while checking to see if he closes his eyes—if he's in love.

When she gets back home at the end of July, she finds two letters that he has sent in advance, bursts into tears in front of her startled mother, and never replies to them. Then she is engaged all summer to a wonderful boy with green eyes called André; his father is a famous surgeon who successfully sewed back on a boy's hand, which had been severed by a chain saw, and who drives a sky blue Buick without a single glance at the surrounding common folk; while they show each other the whites of their tanned bodies behind the sand dunes.

BUT, IN HER HEART of hearts, there is only one real childhood fiancé, a little before adolescence, she's twelve, he's sixteen maybe, but she's already reading and rereading Racine out loud. He has only one arm, the left one was cut off just below the shoulder, but she doesn't know why, nor can she explain the constant return during those years of *the armless man,* and how that missing element nurtures her desire—to cradle, embrace, hug. Is love born of what is impossible? Is love what you can only ever keep in sight?

She watches him as he strides alongside the swimming pool with the splendor of his tanned body, a bathrobe constantly draped over his left shoulder, which he drops to the ground with practiced ease at the very moment when he slips his entire body into the blue water for long periods, leaving as his only trace that pale heap of toweling on the tiles, which she recognizes from afar and keeps in her sights, until he heaves himself back up into the air—his shoulders, his back—and strolls off again, a draped and wounded god among the sunbathing swimmers.

Sometimes their eyes meet. He then smiles at her openly, but she scarcely responds and remains haughty, scared that a sweeter response will change the violent love in her heart into vulgar pity.

Then, one day—she's leaving the next day to stay with her pen pal in London—she lets herself go and, after the pool, in the throes of approaching exile, she attaches a little note signed with her name, which he presumably doesn't know, to the brakes of the moped that she's seen him drive so skillfully: "I really love you."

The wind probably blew it away. During the rest of that summer, she tells all the English boys that she's got a lovely fiancé with only one arm—a boyfriend, you mean? No, I mean a fiancé.

AT THIS POINT in the story, she'd like to make an exception to the rules of the novel. Maybe she doesn't want this man to seem imaginary, the wound he left certainly wasn't. So she'd like to write down his name, his real name, which she's never forgotten: it's almost certainly wrong of her, as wrong as not responding to his smile, but isn't writing sometimes precisely about making up for your mistakes, and for love letters blown away in the wind?

Régis Arbez, I really loved you.

The Father

WHEN HER SISTER is fourteen and she's twelve, the father explains everything: blood, periods, where it comes from, why, the uterus, Fallopian tubes, ovaries, he draws a diagram on a sheet of paper, here's the vagina, here's the cervix, if the egg isn't fertilized (he says: "the egg," she pictures an egg), then the lining peels and flakes away and the womb is let down and bleeds. (He says: "let down," she imagines you feel sad on those days.)

Her sister asks how the egg gets fertilized (she knows, of course, but asks anyway). So the father explains everything: the penis, the foreskin, the urethra, he draws another diagram, the spermatozoa, where they come from, where they go.—Oh, really? But how?— I'll explain again, the father says. Look, here's the penis ("Is that the same as a dick?" she butts in—"No, don't start mixing things up"), so, anyway, the penis enters the vagina, in what is called intercourse. Then the man sends his spermatozoa into the urethra in what is called ejaculation. Then he withdraws ("What a letdown"—"Look, if you keep interrupting like that, I'll stop"). There are then two possibilities: either it's the right day for the woman and she can be fertilized—and have a baby—or she isn't ovulating and so can't become pregnant. If it's the right day, the spermatozoa surround the egg and the fastest one goes inside in what is called conception. The fertilized egg then lodges in the uterus and the baby grows there for nine months, in what is called gestation. When the nine months are up, it comes out in what is called parturition.

"And what is it?" she asks. "A boy?"

The father answers, he's forgotten to tell them about that, so he explains, the father knows absolutely everything, about chromosomes, genetics, XX, XY, and probability. Any other questions?

Her sister has one: she wants to know which the right days are.

She knows, so she puts up her hand, like at school: it's the XY days—no, it isn't, she hasn't understood a single word—zero out of twenty for carnal knowledge.

The father starts off again about menstruation, cycles lasting approximately twenty-eight days, which days are the right ones for getting pregnant, assuming you want to get pregnant of course, in other words only if you're married: because young girls have irregular cycles, so there's no way of telling exactly, and the business about counting from the eighth to the sixteenth day doesn't really work, they can get pregnant at any time, that's the danger, that's why he's doing all this explaining, so that they will understand that, for them, every day is right—in other words, every day is wrong.

And while we're at it, we might as well go the whole hog: the first time, you can even get pregnant during your period, even when using a condom (the father says "a rubber johnny," but they know about them, they found one once in their mother's bedside table, it unfolds like the finger of a glove), it can even happen if they're on the pill. You can even wind up with a bun in the oven without full penetration, if their partner ejaculates on the lips of the vagina, even if they're still virgins the spermatozoa can cross over the hymen and there you are, even from sitting down on a dirty toilet seat, from wiping themselves on a towel, if there's just one drop of sperm, that's enough, things like that can happen so quickly, so very very quickly.

So it's strictly forbidden to be naked with a boy unless you're married. You say no, you clamp your knees together, and keep your pants on, in what is called abstinence.

"HAVE YOU HEARD this one?" she says to her sister on the way back from Sunday school. "It's a prayer I've just learned, which Catholics say: 'Oh, Virgin Mary, you who had one without doing it, please let me do it without having one.'"

It's definitely blasphemous, but she doesn't care. She's a Protestant.

Alone with Him

"SHE MADE A happy man of me," "At last, she agreed to make me a happy man," as they say in eighteenth-century novels. A man's sentence, a true male sentence for you, I wonder if it sins by omission or excess, if it's just a plain euphemism or a vulgar hyperbole, if a man's happiness lies this side of a woman's body, or beyond.

Have you noticed that, in the other direction, the question isn't even raised? "How was it for you? Happy?" cannot be anything more than a derisive joke, as though you weren't even talking about the same thing, the same feelings, as if everything were quite different.

Make me happy, give me what I've given you, give me happiness, is this, do you think, what causes the hysteria of women like me: a sudden cry claiming their due, the taste of happiness in your mouth, kiss me, look at me, I want to be happy—that surge from the body demanding something from another's body that lies beyond its knowledge, that is neither pleasure, nor an orgasm, but happiness, quite simply happiness?

The First Love

SHE FIRST GETS interested in him when she sees him in a photo. He's been there in the flesh before her very eyes for the past fortnight, but she first discovers him in a picture: "What about him over there, with his back turned, who's he?" she asks a girlfriend who's developed the pictures she's taken of their first week by the sea. The friend giggles: "OK, I know they're in black and white, but really!" Then, before her silent curiosity, she cries out: "Can't you see? It's Michel!"

It's Michel. Shoulders at once curved and square, straight neck below his curls, powerful back thinning like a V into his waist, and those arms, thin but muscular. It's Michel.

Yes, oh yes, oh yes.

SINCE THE BEGINNING of the vacation, she's already been out with two boys—two summer flings, as her mother would put it (at home, when the father's not there, they listen to Michel Delpech, but here, in the campsite by the dunes, it's more the Doors, the Who, Jefferson Airplane). She now has to get rid of them, both of them. One evening, she pretends to get drunk so she can go wild and do what she really wants—there will always be a chance to forget later.

But, the next day, Michel is the one who remembers nothing. He apologizes: "I drank too much."

She has to refresh his memory: "You know we kissed last night. Several times."

Oh yes we did, oh yes we did.

She wants to start again, to carry on. She's in love with him. All her friends think he's ugly. He's got bright red hair, almost orange, with milky skin that peels instead of tans. When he was little, everyone called him Red or Ginger or Carrot Top. And they still do. His friends chant after him: "Better dead than a redhead." Then they ask her if he's naturally ginger. She blushes.

HE HAS BEAUTIFUL lips, his hands and skin are soft. She likes the fact that he doesn't say much, that he bursts out laughing, and that he gets excellent grades at school. She loves his redness, his freckles, his resistance to others' stares—what does she care about boys who have never suffered? He's like no one else, he's different from the others, he is other, the other person in whom you recognize yourself—isn't being that other person something special?

She loves him like no one else.

HE MAY BE a natural redhead, but she doesn't know that yet. Her father has authorized this vacation by the sea under the supervision of a friend's family and with certain conditions: no boys in the tent, no outings except in a group. "Because," he said during the final briefing—choosing an expression she found rather trivial for such a weighty matter—"Because," he said solemnly, "if you heat a chestnut long enough, it goes pop."

———

THREE MONTHS LATER, he admits that he lied to her, that he'd never had a real girlfriend before her, he was just bragging, in fact, he's like her, he's never, you know, he's still a virgin.

He's a virgin. And this is harder to live with than being a red-head. But it doesn't last as long.

THE DAY WHEN they make love for the first time, she writes it all down in her diary. But, because she suspects that they read it when she's out, she decides to frame her account as if it was one of the extracts from novels that she often copies out among her letters and her favorite poems. She writes it down in inverted commas and in the third person singular and, just as she has noted down Paul Éluard or Guillaume Apollinaire elsewhere, she rounds it off with a name she makes up, a pseudo eponym, the name of a fictional author who, although she doesn't yet know it, actually exists and whom she will later read with great enthusiasm. She thinks for a while, then signs: Claude Simon.

SO THE FIRST LOVE is caught forever in the web of words, in the tightly woven fabric of sentences. A forbidden act, finding its expression. She's fifteen. She has now stopped simply living her life out, she's started creating it, molding it, inventing it. For the first time, she's in love and writing. In her hands, she has a man and a book. For the first time.

The Teacher

HIS BODY IS large and unharmonious, a long torso over short legs and a face of extraordinary sensuality—thick lips, eyes almost sunk into his features and seeming to try to emerge from them, the dark scruffy hair of a crazed musician: the overall effect is hard to take in, hard to look at for long. His appearance seems to have been foisted on him by nature and when he arrives without a tie some mornings or in the summer without a jacket, under his shirt you can make out a dark fleece covering his entire torso.

She's seventeen, and still with Michel, who's preparing the entry exam to the prestigious École Polytechnique. She's in her last year of high school and spends hours every week watching the teacher—she also listens to him, but firstly, and passionately, she looks at him. She observes every detail, plunges into endless speculations, into a real semiology of the body. Why does the teacher have such powerful, earthy hands, and the arms of a lumberjack—so much so that there's nothing intellectual about him, not a single sign of sensitivity when he isn't talking? And those scratches on his rather pudgy cheek, were they made by a cat, a razor, or a rabid lover? He doesn't wear a wedding ring, he arrives from Paris by train every Monday. And what about that apelike, vibrant mess of a face, which he makes a spectacle of every day in the only all-girls class in school, is that really desire you can read on it—crazy, uncontrollable desire that's stronger than he is—or just the torment of having an intellect in perpetual motion? She wonders. Sometimes, after leaving Michel's arms, whose pale almost hairless skin she has caressed, she thinks of the teacher as a sort of grotesque caricature of manliness. But then he starts speaking, and the lesson begins, a master class. She observes those rugged hands as they grapple after thought, that massive body tussling with ideas, she hears that deep voice intoning the reflections of its mind, then stupefying, absolute, unsustainable beauty suddenly appears. She can see it, she wants it, it's beauty that pains her, that overwhelms her. She has to look down at her exercise book, stop looking at him, she's frozen as though by some extraterrestrial's laser beam. The teacher is no longer a caricature, but the pure essence of the male sex. She looks at him again and, as he wipes his brow and falls silent, she says to herself, as if it were for the first time, as if she's never seen one before, as if it were a discovery, she says: "This is a man."

JUST BEFORE the Easter holidays, he enters her in the interschool prize competition; he speaks to her for a long time in the library where she works after lessons; he buys her a cup of coffee or hot chocolate at the vending machine; he lends her books. One day, at noon, he asks her out to lunch. She accepts, but says that she has to go and tell her grandmother, whom she usually has lunch with on weekdays, and get her things for afternoon lessons. When she comes back, breathless, he's sitting on the wall seat in the restaurant, he looks up from the menu and his face twists into a sort of radiant joy. "Have you been running?" he asks—as though saying, with equal gratitude: "Do you love me, then?" Then he orders and eats enough for a brigade.

On another occasion, she bumps into him in a bookshop. He's browsing through a work about Botticelli, and he tells her she is Spring. He buys the book then gives her a copy of Saint-John Perse's poetry. They discuss the scandal going on in a nearby school—the firing of a teacher and the expulsion of a girl pupil. He comes down extremely hard on this subject and emphasizes his point by frequently using the word "deontology," she doesn't know what it means—that evening, she looks it up in her dictionary—but she agrees. She feels disappointed (the previous year, she'd been smitten by the beautiful eyes of a history teacher, until the day when, just before the end of term, she saw him park a spanking new camping car with a deal of difficulty in the school parking lot. Here, it's rather similar; the grapes wither on the vine).

"And on the strand of my body, the seaborn man lies down. May he freshen his face in the very source of the sands; may he delight in my territory like the tattooed god of the male fern . . . Are you thirsty, my love? I am a woman to your lips who is newer than thirst. And my face in your hands, as though in the cool hands of the shipwreck, ah! in this warm night may you have freshness of almond and flavor of dawn, and just knowledge of the fruit of the strange shore."

She reads aloud to herself in her bedroom. Whatever he mentions, or alludes to, she reads. She wants to know what he thinks, what he loves, what he is. How it is that one man can unite ugliness and seductiveness, piggishness and eloquence, desire and deontology (the camping car and those eyes), she wants to know how such a thing is possible. Often, when she goes back to her grandmother's, she finds her listening to favorite songs on an old gramophone: "Pleasure of Love" or "Paradise Lost," or, more recently, a refrain that she hums while setting the table: "Ain't it nice in the arms of the opposite sex Ain't it nice in those arms Ain't it nice in the arms of another kind from you Ain't it nice in those arms." She sings along with her grandmother, waltzing her around while thinking of the teacher. He isn't her kind, really. But that's just the point . . . that's what fascinates her. Another, the opposite sex, the strange shore. Definitely not her kind. Another kind from her.

Alone with Him

DO YOU KNOW Saint-John Perse? And *Amers* in particular? The collection of his called *Amers?* It's a dialogue between two lovers, a naked couple in an oceanic bedroom—I don't even know if you like poetry (you certainly like the ocean, your waiting room is plastered with seascapes). What's special about it is the absolutely extraordinary emphasis placed on the difference between the sexes: the fleeting, almost unbearable physical union of two bodies that are separated by everything except desire—the desire to enter what has been opened, the desire to open and be seen to be open—the shared desire to struggle against death. That's all. What's the rest about? The sea and the shore, strength and sweetness, power and obedience, the hunter and the gentle beast, lightning and the pomegranate, silence and the scream, the wandering soul and the resident heart, the pilot and the craft, the traveler and the home, the master and the maid, the wing and the bed. Male and female. Night and day.

So the only time they find each other is in the act of love, or what we call love, that dividing line between earth and water, that frail horizon between the sea and the sky, that's where they find each other, as dancers, tightrope walkers, close, near, nearer still in that relationship, that sexual relationship, the only one that has any meaning, without which no other relationship exists. We're alone. There is no point in asking questions or calling out. *"Where are you? the dream says. For you live so far away . . . and me, do I know the way to reach you? O beloved face, far from my doorway . . . Where are you fighting so far away that I am absent? For what cause other than mine? Where are you? the dream says.*

"And you, you have no answer."

SO WHY ARE you still so distant? Why are you still drawn elsewhere, and to which elsewhere? Why? Does this journey in fact have any purpose, a goal? Were you really born of the sea and want to voyage ever onward? Are you really that pure-browed nomad "haunted by things distant and great"? What things, why, what are you thinking about? Is your world larger than the silence in which I'm calling out? Are you strong, are you noble, are you proud? What of, and why? What is your nature and where is my love directed? To an athlete's body, a master's oppression, or a god's jealousy? Are you powerful, are you weak? Do you exist without me, without my love? Do you really? And if the sea washes you away, where do you go where I am not, to what place unknown to me? Is it a journey or trickery, an illusive departure? Are you really going? And if the sea washes you away, will death wash you back? Are you coming back? Will you come back? Where from? Where do you come from when you're on your way, when you say: "I'm on my way"? Does it take that long, is it that far? "Footfalls are fading inside me," are they yours? Where are you going? Where are you? Who are you?

AND YOU, you have no answer.

The First Love

FOR A LONG TIME, she stays with her first love. Every Saturday, she goes to the movies with him then, dawdling on his motorbike, they go home together, either to his place or to hers. On Sundays, they make love in the afternoon while their parents are out. They go on vacation together, and as soon as Michel passes his test, they travel around in a little Renault, they go to Venice, to Ljubljana, to Amsterdam, to London, they smoke dope, they attend Jim Morrison's funeral, they kiss on the Bridge of Sighs, they demonstrate with the Planned Parenthood association, they go to a Weather Report concert in Châteauvallon, they play darts in pubs in Inverness, they tread in James Joyce's footsteps in Dublin, they visit Freud's house in Vienna: they're in love.

ONE DAY—its December 31, not just any old day—she waits for him, he doesn't come. He calls rather late to say that he isn't coming, that he's not too keen on compulsory festivities, that he's also got some really tough math homework to do, that he's going to finish it, then go to bed.

There are boys she finds attractive at the party where she goes alone, but not one of them speaks to her or asks her to dance: she's with Michel.

When she gets back home, she writes in her diary:

> So cry cry and cry again
> Whether the moon is full
> Or still a mere crescent
> Oh, cry cry and cry again
> We laughed so much in the sun
>
> Arms of gold bear up life
> Penetrate the gilded secret
> Life is just a vapid flame
> Which brings out the lovely rose
> Wafting its delicious scent

TWO WEEKS LATER, she locks herself in her bedroom, puts on Leonard Cohen, and swallows all the pills she can find in the medicine cabinet. She sits on her bed holding a blank piece of paper, but nothing comes, not a single word to express it all—that she needs arms of gold to bear life. She listens to Cohen's voice: *I need you, I don't need you,* she can no longer live or die.

She takes her bike to Michel's house, he's in, his mother calls to him, he comes downstairs (maybe there's someone else in his bedroom?). So she tells him that she's taken some sleeping tablets, that what she really wanted to do was have an accident on the way there, that was what she was hoping for. He goes as white as death, as white as the sheet of paper that she was incapable of writing anything on, he gets his car keys and yells to his mother: "I'm going with her."

She cries next to him while he's putting her bike into the trunk of the Renault. "I'm going with her." She doesn't even have a name anymore, she sobs, she latches onto his arm, what's wrong Michel? What's happened? What have I done to you? Michel, do you love me? He takes her back home, nothing, nothing at all, just leave me alone, he explains everything to her mother, who calls André, who comes running—but it doesn't seem serious, it's nothing, nothing at all.

That evening, Michel phones and asks her politely if she's OK. "Fine," she says (the father is in the living room reading the paper: when you've got nothing to say, you say nothing). "After what you've just done to me," Michel adds—his final exams are coming— "I think we'd better stop here, and never see each other again."

She doesn't respond—*Seven swords of melancholy With no ivory oh clear agony Are in my heart*—he hangs up.

What you've just done to me.

SHE CRIES OVER meals, she cries for weeks on end. "That's just what boys are like," says the father, who didn't hear the chestnut go pop, "at that age, they all have one-track minds. But don't worry, in the end, it's girls like you they marry."

Girls like you.

THREE MONTHS LATER, she disguises her handwriting and sends Michel a letter signed with an illegible name. It's from a boy who's passionately in love with her, but also utterly desperate because, as he writes pathetically: "She loves only you, she wants only you." And, he goes on: "How can you not respond to that love, she is so beautiful, so wonderful, there are not many girls like her in the world, I do not understand, I really do not, I would give anything to be in your shoes, to be loved by her as she loves you."

Girls like her.

MICHEL RECEIVES the letter one day before a rock concert she knows he's going to attend; she's going there, too, with three boys—safety in numbers. At one point, Michel comes over to her—they haven't spoken since *what you've just done to me,* she's seen him a couple of times with a girl in his car—he tells her that he can't get her out of his mind, that he loves her, that he's sure of that now. She doesn't ask what caused this revelation, she smiles at him.

Men like them.

THAT EVENING, she writes in her diary: "Deception, trickery, and betrayal: the secrets of love."

But, in fact, the secret she has discovered is quite different—the secret of language. Truth is whatever can be written down. On the turntable, Léo Ferré is singing: "Weapons and words, they're the same, they kill just the same." But those words that grab another person at a distance, wherever he happens to be, like a hand on his shoulder, can also restore life.

The Teacher

SHE AND THE TEACHER are sitting on the sofa. She bumped into him at the movies, where she'd gone with her sister, then invited him back for some orange juice—all the cafés being closed.

The teacher looks around at everything eagerly: the strict furniture, the paintings of local landscapes, the handful of hardcover books on the glazed shelves, and, in perspective down the corridor, the parents' bedroom, the entire surface area taken up by an austere bed of dark oak, flanked by two bedside tables with matching lamp shades, an ironic image of the couple. "What an extraordinarily Protestant interior," the teacher says, a fan of Barthes and the semiology of daily life. "If I hadn't known you were Protestant, I'd have guessed from the furnishings . . . so cold and austere."

"Oh, do you think so (*and what about me, do I look Protestant too*)?"

At that moment, her mother comes back from the restaurant with André, they greet the teacher, "Good evening," "Good evening," then disappear into the bedroom, the door of which closes on their rather tipsy laughter.

"We're disturbing your parents," the teacher says, his eyes fixed on the keyhole that has remained dark.

"Oh no, that isn't my father," she replies.

He glances around at her with a flash of naked, violent, vulgar desire in his eyes, then, since she's so politely holding out a bowl of pistachios, he takes a handful and thanks her. But his gaze keeps returning to that closed door, he looks rather distant, as though dreaming of some future perspective.

Protestant maybe. Catholic not.

The Father

THE FATHER ISN'T father to everyone. To others he's a boss, an acquaintance, a friend, a lover. To her mother, he's a husband. But it's the same man, it's always him.

"JUST IMAGINE, it was three days after the wedding, we were on our honeymoon in Venice, I'd decided to go to the hairdresser's to make myself beautiful for him, and the hotel hairdresser suggested I should try a new look, a more modern hairstyle—I had long hair that didn't really suit me—anyway, you see, I was only nineteen, I said OK. And when I went back to him . . . When I went back! Your father, who wasn't your father yet, at the time, went wild, I mean really wild. He was furious, livid, he blamed me for not asking his opinion, accused me of disobeying him—he's supposed to have told me to keep my hair long—anyway, to make a long story short, he didn't speak to me for two weeks. Can you imagine that? For two weeks, on our honeymoon! I cried and I cried and I cried! I was only nineteen, you know, I'd just left my father and mother.

"Then there was the time when I had my lymphangitis—I'd

just had your sister, and God was I in pain! Well, during the night he turned around to face the wall and said: 'Can't you just let me get some sleep?' He was hard when I stop and think, really hard and selfish. I should have left him then and there. I should have gone, that's what I should have done.

"You see, my darling, what really disgusts me is that he's never given me a red cent, no presents, nothing. Nor to you, for that matter, even though you are his daughters . . . When he started out, he didn't have a penny to his name, don't forget that, it was my father who paid for everything: the surgery, the instruments, the car, the flat, he had nothing—his own father was a locksmith, so as you can imagine, he wasn't exactly Louis XVI, he was just a two-bit locksmith. So the least he could have done was to be a bit grateful, I mean, use the money to make us happy, just that! Not a bit of it! It really breaks my heart when I think of my father slaving away to keep his company afloat, and all for his darling little girl.

"So you can imagine that with André, everything was perfect right from the start. He's always been sweet and gentle. As for your father, it's always been in, out, and good night. I was young, my father had always doted on me, spoiled me, I needed affection and I wasn't getting any; in the end, your father has never really given me anything, you see, I know it's terrible to say it to you, but after twenty years of marriage, I don't have a single happy memory. Not one. Except for you two, of course, my daughters. You're the only good thing I've ever done with him.

"So, it's all very well talking about remaining faithful. But faithful to what?"

THE FATHER AND the mother never talk to each other directly. She and her sister transmit their messages and replies. After twenty years, at the end of a meal, the mother asks for a divorce (she has

decided to marry André, and he reciprocally). This request is un-
expected because she hasn't asked for anything for so long. The father has given her two daughters, period. But, that day, she forces
his hand and, even though in his soul his ancestors protest (French
Protestants don't divorce), he agrees.

Alone with Him

YOU WANT ME to say what I know? From experience? Observation? Memory? Or intuition? What life has taught me? Or books? Public and private hearsay?

THAT MEN LISTEN to the radio much louder than we do. That they slam doors. That they don't close cupboards. That they don't know where the saucepans, plates, and oyster forks are kept. That they forget important dates. That they think they have no faults. That they don't experience birth, that they suffer horribly and forget to live. That darkness disturbs them. That they're farsighted but can't find the butter in the fridge. That they make faithful friends. That they sit with their legs splayed. That they say on average seven thousand words per day (and women twenty thousand). That they disassociate love and sex. That they never put the top back on the toothpaste. That they hate umbrellas, even when it's raining. That they aspire to virtue but not to truth. That they're better at mathematical thought. That they have a better sense of direction. That they find it hard to cry. That they build themselves up on negations. That their sensitivity is man's best-kept secret. That they're fragile. That they dislike showing their emotions. That they aren't free not to do what gives them more pleasure than anything else. That they're afraid of not getting an erection. That they accept their feminine side better than they used to. That they forget half the shopping (because they didn't take the list). That they drop their newspapers on the floor when they've finished reading them. That they say to themselves: "Will she find me attractive? Will she love me?" That they buy clothes without trying them on first. That they're no longer indifferent to makeup. That they prefer vacuuming to dusting. That they prefer walking a baby to changing it. That they never forget to call their mothers. That they're all slaves. That few of them reward study. That the world hardens their hearts. That they wouldn't survive long in society if they didn't deceive one another. That they're now changing. That they're better at proposing measures than following them. That they have a tendency to forget both good turns and insults. That they like stockings that stay up on their own. That they prefer brunettes. That they're unenthusiastic when carrying out a duty. That they rarely fail in their suicide attempts. That they would like a quiet life. That men are like that. That they display their hardness, their ingratitude, their unfairness, their pride, their narcissism, and their forgetfulness of others. That this is the way they're made, their nature.

The Abortionist

SHE GETS UP at six in the morning so as not to be disturbed or caught. Every thirty seconds, she looks at the vial—nothing—then, suddenly, there it is, the brown ring, just as it says in the leaflet. She's pregnant.

She contemplates suicide, but doesn't want to die. And, as she did promise Michel to call as soon as she knows, she awaits eight o'clock anxiously.

"I'm coming," he says. "What a pair of early morning love-birds," says her grandmother, whom she's been staying with at the end of that summer, since her parents separated.

"I'm coming," says the family GP to her emergency call, just as a mother says to her child when it calls to her "I'm coming," or as men say when they're about to orgasm.

THEY GO OUT of town and stop beside a lonely wood where they've never been before. Michel isn't the father, he knows that: they haven't made love for months and, during the vacation, they slept together like children, snuggled up in the yellow double bed in the house in the south. She just went away for a couple of days to bring around, as she put it, a rejected suitor who was threatening to kill himself if she refused to see him, even just for an hour—"No, of course I don't sleep with him, and I'm not about to start, anyway, look, I'm not even going to take my diaphragm, I'll leave it here on the bedside table, that way you'll be sure . . ."

She takes the train, suddenly full of violent desire for that other man, who's been calling her every evening, pleading with her to come see him, she's on the train, her stomach a knot of desire digging at her like an insistent voice—fuck him, lay him, get this game of hide-and-seek over once and for all. It's nearly dark by the time she arrives at the station, but it's still hot and sultry. He's waiting for her, she says: "There, in your car, come on." They make love savagely, they fuck, the night is fragrant like a body, there was never any question of death.

"SO YOU DON'T use any means of contraception?" the doctor asks.

"Um, yes, I mean, I had a diaphragm, but apparently it didn't work."

She lies, she senses that it's better this way—there are men you have to lie to.

"A diaphragm? But that's grotesque for a young lady like you. I don't know who prescribed it, but I only recommend it for women who are more . . . Anyway, it's awkward to use, and the failure rate is high—as you yourself now know. Statistically . . ."

(Statistically, a diaphragm in its box three hundred miles away from the scene of the action has never been much use. She bows her head.)

"Now, now, don't get upset. I'll explain what's going to happen."

The syringe. Suction. The technique. Anesthesia. No, she doesn't want to be put to sleep, she wants to be present. The risks.

She signs a form discharging him of all responsibility in case of death. She's been of age since the election of President Giscard d'Estaing, and is now acting legally thanks to Simone Veil's new law, passed just a few months earlier, legalizing abortion. She's lucky.

He tells her that it's going to hurt, but the pain is bearable, rather like what you feel when giving birth—she must have a blank expression on her face, because he adds in embarrassment: "Of course, that doesn't mean much to you. Nor to me, for that matter," he concludes with a smile. "You'll be all right."

At no time is she really frightened. She's at the heart of an enormous paradox, which means that during the anxious moments before the event, the only thing that comforts her is the loving, friendly, reassuring thought of the child, as though she were carrying both life and death.

SHE TRIES to pay the receptionist for the consultation. "You didn't pay the doctor directly?" she's asked. No, she thought that . . . The secretary knocks on the consulting room door to ask.

"No," the doctor's voice says. "I don't want her to . . ."

Then, as though correcting himself.

"No, she'll pay later."

SHE THOUGHT that she'd never forget that man's name. But she's forgotten everything about him, his last name, first name, his face. He must be retired by now, perhaps even dead. She just remembers his voice, the softness of that voice postponing an un-

known feeling of suffering, which he knew would come, which
was bound to come one day—later, much later.

THE CHILD—a girl? a boy?—would now be as old as she was
then.

The Teacher

THE DAY SHE PASSES her final exams, he gives her Yves Nat's recording of Beethoven's piano sonatas. They have tea together across the road from the school. Michel comes along after his last lesson. The next day, they're leaving for Scotland. The teacher extends his hand, have a nice holiday then, thanks, you too. She watches him walk away along Boulevard Jean-Jaurès; for June, there are already a lot of dead leaves.

SHE NEXT SEES HIM two years later in a bookshop in the Latin Quarter, her heart skips a beat when she spots him facing a shelf, his back turned to her, his brow bent over a dictionary, she recognizes his stocky figure, his hair, it's him, she's sure of it. When she's just about to go, he turns around suddenly, as though answering her call.

He's an assistant lecturer at Nanterre University, she's redoing her preparatory year for the entry exams for the École Normale Supérieure. Her studio apartment is nearby. They go there. She's surprised he has condoms with him.

Later that night, he asks if he can use the phone. She goes to the bathroom and overhears him saying that he won't be back—till to-morrow, he says, till tomorrow.

She doesn't understand. She's seized by a vague fear.

BUT NOTHING'S WRONG. The teacher quite simply lives with his mother.

HE LEAPS UP in the middle of dinner; he has to make a phone call. He cancels a weekend away, postpones an evening out, cuts short a date, stands her up. He wonders if this shade of green will suit Her, if She likes the scent of gardenias, if She would like to see this film, this play, this opera, if She would care to go to Bruges, Vienna, Bénodet.

SHE SLEEPS BADLY, loses weight, she cries.

BUT NOTHING'S WRONG. The teacher quite simply loves his mother.

The Father

from here on in
it gets on my tits
you'll grow out of it before I do it again
pass the Kleenexes
I couldn't give a two-bit flying fuck with a cherry on top
a hole rimmed with hairs
to screw yourself ball-less
the family jewels
roast a chestnut long enough, it goes pop
a dickhead
eyes like pissholes in the snow
a cauliflower fanny
everything is contained in everything else and vice versa
I'm against everyone who's for and for everyone who's against
it isn't worth a rabbit's fart
the cat crept into the crypt crapped and crept out again
He bent our ears with his bent mike
nothing like a cock's tube for added flavor

as the actress said to the bishop
a fat lot of good
A speech from the Great Leader who stands out from afar:
"My fellow compatriots,
I've stuck you up to your necks in the poo
But as I am far taller than you
I'm only in it to my knees
Now kindly wipe your arses please."
Whore-daughter!
My hero father, with his gentle smile
fat guts
the payoff
one size fits all
why are you coffin?
"I told those little golden fruit
You're nothing but peanuts."
"One day in a valley
A snake stung Jean Ferry.
And guess what occurred?
The snake was interred."
Individual freedom stops where the next man's starts
You never sit anywhere but on your butt
What's well conceived is well expressed
And the words to say it are easily found.
"A rich bumpkin
On his way out
Summoned his sprogs
And patois did spout."
You don't read at table.
What's the dowager on about?
You were still in your dad's bollocks.
Look at me when I'm talking to you.

When you have nothing to say, you say nothing.
You should never judge your parents.
That's what I think, and I share my opinion.
No comment.
Period.

Alone with Him

I TRIED SOMETHING out yesterday, based on a memory test you do at school: I wrote down all of the expressions people close to me use, or have used often enough or portentously enough for me to remember. See what I mean? I started with my father, and they came so easily I didn't even have to search for them, in just ten minutes I'd covered two whole pages with his turns of phrase, quotations, the jokes he used to make when I was little. Then I read through them. It was as if I was expecting to find some kind of secret buried there, a magic spell containing my father's essence. But instead, it was just awful! Suddenly, our lives are reduced to almost nothing. If I read it to you, you'd see what I mean.

After that, I was incapable of adding another line to his portrait in words—in words so utterly his that they took my own words right out of my mouth. I was dumbstruck, terrified, as though on the brink of an abyss.

I thought that, for a man who said nothing, two pages were quite a lot, that it would flesh out his mystery and reveal his secret. Then it felt as though a pit had opened in my soul, because what my little pile of crumbs did suddenly reveal was that there wasn't any secret, not the slightest trace of one in fact. The father isn't *my hero*, and that's an end to it, happy are you?—"you must kill the father" and all that crap? But I'm not going to leave it there, as you put it, I'm going to carry on. You'll see.

The Father

SHE WRITES because he says nothing. In an interview she once said: "In my family, we're not very talkative."

And yet he does speak. The proof is that she can remember. She's written it all down. She's printed it out.

She reads over what she's written—or rather, what he's said, she rereads what she's written down of what he's said.

She compares it with the mother's expressions; no matter how hard she tries, she can remember just two: "sweetheart" and "my love" (and then, in her presence, but addressed to André, that strange word her mother used when talking to her Man, that foreign language of love, that mysterious tongue she would learn later, of course, that sound whose hidden meaning is so easy to guess, even when you're six: *darling*).

As for André, apart from "my lovely," only one more springs to mind: a judgmental, tragic expression, like those sentences that linger after awaking from a nightmare that has otherwise been totally forgotten, and which he pronounces when she and her sister, alarmed by the screaming, rush into the living room in their nightgowns, a pair of white bats out of hell, to find André sitting placidly in one of the Louis XVI wing chairs, while the mother is busy throwing the remaining chairs over the balcony without even checking if anyone is walking below—just one phrase, elaborated in this mayhem, set off for some reason that remains a mystery to her (an abortion maybe, but she digs no deeper into women's mysteries, she doesn't have time, there are too many men), just one sentence, clear and concise, which seems to sum up what all men think of all women, and this is why she can remember it: "Your mother's nuts."

BUT IT'S DIFFERENT when it comes to the father, there are so many of them, and still more are coming back to her—if you're happy, laugh a while; how do you make a Venetian blind? I took my wife to the station to see the engines shunt, and when she wasn't looking the sparks flew up her, Country girls are pretty. . . .

SHE READS them again and, yes, there is a secret after all. But what is it?

THEN SHE UNDERSTANDS: the father's secret is his language—dirty talk, locker-room humor, schoolboy jokes, juvenile puns on sex and women, a male language. The father speaks to her like this when she's little, so she can learn it, so she can soak it up. He's had only girls, but he talks to them as if they were boys, man to man, with that added hint of childishness, that naïve humor that apparently also appeals to the girlies.

Is that how men speak? It must be, because that's how the father speaks.

Men don't talk about love—they don't say "sweetheart" or "my love."

Men don't feel sorry for themselves, they just have a laugh: "Go on, have a good sob, that way you'll piss less."

Men don't use the flowery language of effeminate metaphors and romantic figures of speech: tiny golden fruit are just peanuts and women are holes rimmed with hairs. Who cares about the poetry of intellectuals? You don't look at the mantelpiece when you're poking the fire, and the words to say it are easily found.

IT'S LANGUAGE in its crude state, with balls.

CAMILLE LEARNS IT quickly. So does her sister, Claude. No screams, no tears. That's girls' stuff. I'll make a man of you, my girl. And when you have nothing to say, you say nothing.

SHE REREADS what she's written, then rereads her previous three novels. It's clear that the father has given her his language, a virile voice that haunts the text, giving it a male ring, he's the creator of it, her creator. Isn't the father her hero? He's certainly the hero of the story. When she writes, he directs, she writes in his language, in her father tongue.

Alone with Him

MY MOTHER TONGUE? You want to hear it, do you?

Well, you will. I promise you that.

But do you really want to hear it? Is this just plain curiosity? Aren't you afraid, aren't you scared of a voice that yells? Aren't you frightened of love, of women's love?

The Teacher

SHE AND THE TEACHER plan to go away on holiday together. But he will probably have to back down, as he explains one evening after she's already bought a summer dress and a guidebook to the Cyclades, because, as he points out, unlike her, he doesn't really have the means to go—what with the rent for his three-room flat in the sixth arrondissement, his mother, the books he has to buy for his thesis, so, if he can't find someone to lend him the money, she'll have to go on her own.

She empties the savings account her grandmother used to be so proud of, buys their plane tickets, and gives him half of what's left—if he can pay her back in three months' time, then that will be fine, because she's thinking of moving out of her tiny attic bedsit into a larger place with a kitchen and an inside toilet. He says "surely" and insists on drawing up a repayment schedule.

HIS MOTHER GOES to the airport with them. "Careful," the teacher told her the evening before, "not too many ribbons and bows—you can only take forty-five pounds in luggage." So she arrives in Orly with her bag almost empty—after all, when it's sunny, you can go practically naked. The teacher has two enormous suitcases and a lot of cumbersome photographic equipment slung over his shoulder—two camera bodies, fifteen lenses, a tripod, six filters—"Are you a top model?" the landlady later asks her with an amazed grin. Before checking in, he stuffs a huge medicine bag and first-aid kit into her bag—"I bet you haven't even brought along any aspirin," he comments indulgently, while looking at his mother knowingly. "Maybe you didn't realize, but if you catch a bug out there and you haven't brought your own antibiotics, then you'll be dead and buried before they have time to airlift you out." His mother asks if she's thought of packing a sewing kit, no, she hasn't, well too bad for her then, let's just hope and pray that she doesn't get blisters, because with no needle . . . Has she at least got a good sturdy pair of hiking boots? It's rocky over there. As for the teacher, he has bought himself an excellent pair, which weigh over three pounds each.

Her heart is fluttering, she can't find her passport, ah yes, here it is. She pays the 350 franc excess baggage charge.

IT'S VERY HOT in Athens. The teacher doesn't want to go to the Acropolis with her, he knows it like the back of his hand, he went there three times when he was a student. But for her, it's the first time; she wanders for ages through the streets, then among the ruins, consulting her tourist guidebook. In the museum, the shard of a vase reminds her of a marvelous lesson the teacher gave about Plato when she was still his student—a vivid lesson, about love.

The next day, they take a boat from Piraeus. On the quay, he talks her out of buying a copper bracelet she likes from a little peddler. They sleep in the steerage, huddled up together in the chill of the night (cabins are rather expensive). On Thira, they rent on a weekly basis an almost empty blue-and-white maisonette full of centipedes. The teacher suggests that they pool their resources, which will facilitate daily spending—she puts all her money into the plastic pouch he wears on his belt. Every evening, after the beach where they eat only bread and tomatoes, because restaurants are a terrible tourist trap, and in any case the teacher could do with losing a few pounds, they walk back to the village before the post office closes. It's a tiny building, perched on the side of the mountain, where, to her amazement, day after day the telephone operator manages to get through to Paris, France, where his mother's not feeling so well.

At night, some nights, they make love, she closes her eyes beneath that huge, powerful body, she raises her pelvis toward his hips and squeezes them, "farther, oh yes, farther" as if he could be any farther—and when he's asleep, she cries.

THEY'VE BEEN THERE for nearly two weeks when she asks to phone her grandmother, who is now alone in Rouen. "OK," the teacher says, frowning. "But not for too long," he then adds, pointing at his pouch.

That evening, she tells him that she's going. The boat leaves at nine P.M. and she's going to take it. "I'm not really surprised," he says. "You're like Mother, you need a comfortable existence." The landlady knocks on the door, it's Saturday and she wants to know if they're staying on or not. The teacher cautiously removes some banknotes from his pouch and pays for another two weeks. When she asks for her share, he tallies up aloud the amount she'll need to get to the airport in Athens—the boat, the cab—because, in any case, you can't change drachmas in France.

On the deck of the boat, she waves. The teacher looks sad and appears amazed to see the hull moving away from the quay. He walks alongside, the wind has risen, and she can't hear what he's shouting across to her as he breaks into a run—something like

"I'm your lover," perhaps? No, it isn't that, she understands when he mimes swallowing something, she shrugs, no, sorry, she has forgotten to leave him the first-aid box.

IN ATHENS, she has five hours to kill before boarding. She puts her bag in a locker and strolls through the streets. She's twenty, she's Spring, all the men hail her, or follow her, she smiles at them in a way she never would in Paris.

At the airport, she calls her grandmother to tell her that she's on her way back. With the few drachmas she has left, she buys a coiled bracelet and slips it straight onto her wrist.

SHE WAITS three months before phoning the teacher. He's out, having dinner somewhere in town. When she mentions the reason for her call, his mother yells down the line: "Oh yes, money! . . . It's always money!"

LATER, SHE LOOKS back at her trip to the Greek islands with purely Hellenic philosophy. In the end, it doesn't really matter, it just means that there's a man out there who owes her something.

Men

WHEN SHE MEETS a man she finds attractive, she never wonders—
and never asks—if he's alone.

All men are alone by definition.

THEY HAVE a mother, a wife—sometimes several wives—children,
friends, acquaintances, and plans for the future. They are attached
to them by ties that in some cases will come undone (if too taut,
they snap, if too loose, they unravel). But it isn't her intention to
set them free, that's not why she's here, and in any case it's beyond
her means. She knows that they're tied, that they're taken ("I love
him, but he's taken," as you can read in letters to agony aunts, as if
somewhere there was a man who's really *free*). So, they're taken,
sometimes even extremely taken ("Sorry, my dear, but I'm extremely taken up right now," as a grand Parisian doctor used to
put it, whose mistress she was for a time, until she started to find
the light from scialytic lamps too clinical). Often, it's precisely
such ties that attract her to a man, she's interested in what a man
adheres to.

And yet, despite these knots, she wants to be able to approach
in a movement evocative of life—the point of attachment mustn't

be too near, nor the rope too short (and some of its threads must have already been severed). Instead of boats firmly moored together and to the quay, she prefers a dinghy bobbing up and down a little farther out on the waves, by the tip of the pier. She knows that it, too, is moored and anchored, but its bobbing conceals that fact.

WHAT SHE LOVES in men is that floating freedom, ties that leave room for maneuver, liberty of movement.

By definition all men are taken. But with some, there's a give-and-take.

Alone with Him

WHAT INTERESTS ME is the difference between the sexes. What I expect from a relationship (and "expect" is just the right word, I'm still expecting) is that this difference draws me closer to him, and at once confirms its existence as a difference while also fading away. Making love means being a woman and being filled by a man—I'm talking about penetration, what I mean is, when you are penetrated, you also penetrate the other's mystery, or at least you hope you can. What's odd is that desire is born of difference, which then, or so it seems to me, progresses toward a cancellation of the difference. What attracts me about a man is that he's a man, and what makes me happy later, in love, is that we're both the same. That's what I expect from a man, a merging together into fusion, a moment when, as the saying goes, *their bodies become one.*

I'VE ALWAYS HAD problems spending much time with someone I have no desire for and who has no desire for me: a woman, for instance, or a homosexual, or a man who stays rooted in his function, his social or professional role, who talks to you from some place outside his body, and alien to yours. I don't like American-style friends at work, their supposedly egalitarian way of treating others as colleagues, comrades, workmates, brothers, and sisters—that fake abolition of otherness that makes everyone so uniform and falsely familiar. For others, I want to be a terra incognita, but not somewhere they dream of occupying like a conquistador, or setting on blaze for all eternity, just something to explore, that's all, something they can finally discover. I love explorers, men who are curious about women and about that part of themselves that, dark, obscure, and desirable, lies in others. You might say, you may very well say (no you won't, you never say anything): "Why the body? Why desire, why sex?"

Because it's a way of knowing, and the best one we have, given that the difference is fundamentally sexual after all! The Bible uses the verb "to know" to mean "to make love" and that says it all: I love men who want to know me.

The Male Friend

THE MALE FRIEND IS an intrinsic rarity. He's more of an abstract figure, an imaginary projection or else a myth adapted as far as possible to fit in with everyday life. The male friend, in fact, does not exist, it's merely a convenient term used to describe certain individuals. In reality, she believes in women's friendship and all she wants from men is love. So there's little room left for a male friend.

Whenever one of his fellows introduced a girl to Stendhal as a "friend," he used to say "what, already?" She's rather similar—friendship for her seems to be more an end than a beginning, but not an end in the sense of a goal to be reached, of course, and even less of a successful conclusion, but an end in the sense of termination: the end. For her, friendship is the end of love, that's all there is to it. The male friend has once been loved and no longer is. He is a dismal manifestation of the passing of time, of time that has passed. She has sometimes said to men and men said to her: "Let's remain friends." What an excellent example of circumlocution: for what more is friendship than remains?

So she is not someone you could describe as having "lots of friends," and she's proud of this fact. Such an illusory possession would in fact reveal everything she has lost, that she no longer has. The male friend is always sad, it's a form of heartbreak.

OR ELSE, the male friend is gay. He takes her to the opera, she invites him to the restaurant, they go to the museum and theater together, they learn how to tango and shop at sales. Sometimes he takes her to the Casa Rosa, a "private gay club," where hundreds of men, and a handful of women that look like them, dance theatrically. There are several rooms, several floors, and raised platforms. The men there are often bare-chested, revealing their perfect bodies in the half-light, their golden arms, shoulders, smooth shiny backs, faces entirely taken up with one another. She suffers a million torments, she could drop dead like an old dog. The friend disappears then comes back, he gives her a hug and asks if she's OK. She says yes, she yells, they can't hear each other.

AT THE CASA ROSA, she's alone, alone to a quite terrifying degree, so alien she could die. Suddenly, it's not such a good idea to be a woman.

The Father

THE FATHER IS special—she sets him apart, as the male part of her. When she gets out of the bath, with her hair plastered down her back, naked skin, no makeup, her features somewhat hardened by the fluorescent light, bushy eyebrows, serious expression, she suddenly sees him in the mirror: it's him.

The father is the only male face a woman has; the father is the only man she's ever allowed to be.

The Husband

THE HUSBAND EXPERIENCES some problems in becoming the husband—he tells her that looking straight into her eyes late one evening at the Closerie des Lilas: he isn't free. He lives nearby with an older woman he's attached to. But he's going to make a break, she's the one he wants to marry; she's the one he adores.

They've known each other for three days. She replies that she isn't free, either: his name's Amal, he's gone to live in New York, where she's supposed to join him, but now she won't go, it's over.

They introduce themselves: she's a dancer and she's also trying to write, she loves Guillaume Apollinaire; he used to be a champion swimmer, he writes poems no one will publish, he loves Yeats, T. S. Eliot, Shakespeare, the theater, he hates this era and drives a white sports car, when he gives her a lift home, she'll understand why. That evening, at the Closerie des Lilas, they linger in delight over their similarities. That night, at her place, a huge thunderstorm breaks out as they kiss—electric nights, magnetic skin. The gods are jealous.

THEY GET MARRIED. He teaches English in Rouen, she's a librarian in Vernon, they live in Paris. They meet up in the train nearly every day—it's the same line—exhausted, smitten, they make love, they never stop.

One Friday, he tells her that he won't be back that evening because he's taking some British colleagues to Le Havre. "I'll miss you," she says, as though talking about the train.

She sits in the carriage and reads the *Le Monde*. Then, suddenly, even though they passed the blocks of council flats in Mantes-la-Jolie long ago—they'll arrive in under ten minutes, the passengers are already gathering by the doors—she picks up her things and sets off up the train against the tide, opens the sliding door, crosses another carriage, then another, and another—"Hey, lady, you're heading the wrong way," says a backpacker, slumped across the aisle, she steps over him and keeps going, she wants to go through the entire train before it arrives, before there's the crush of people getting off, she wants to be sure that she's wrong.

The rear carriages are almost empty, a quick glance is enough to reassure her that nobody's there.

She opens the last sliding door and walks up to the rear window. Through it, you can see the tracks, the road, trees retreating into the distance. And, just beside it, alone, watching the countryside, there he is.

She advances toward him (slap him, rip half his hair out, throw herself off the train), the shadow her body casts makes him look up, he smiles as if he's proud of her, well played "darling"—the husband is extremely "fair play" and a very good "sport." When she reaches him, she throws her bag into his face, bad shot, *mon amour*, take that in the *nez*, *chéri*, never give your whole heart, *la plume de ma tante*, and my *femme* is nuts. Then she faints. Sonofabitch.

Amal

AMAL IS Moroccan, he has a fuzzy black beard and a pronounced oriental appearance, which makes him look like a Khomeini supporter, but which is not the case, far from it . . . The first time she meets him at the Palace, he has the sleepy gaze of a hash smoker, but in the nightclub where all the men are apparently dancing only for themselves thus making her feel invisible, she's grateful to him for not taking his eyes off her. And yet, when she gets her coat back from the cloakroom and he asks for her phone number, she tells it to him only because, she thinks, he's bound to forget it.

THE NEXT DAY, he calls her, he's got two tickets for *Don Giovanni*, would she care to come with him?

Then he has two tickets for *Der Rosenkavalier*. Then they see a production of *Bérénice* that makes her furious, in which Titus is asleep and snoring during the wonderful avowal: "I loved, O lord, I loved, I wanted to be loved." Then she cries at a Léo Nucci concert, and for the death of the Marquis de Posa. Then he invites her to the restaurant, gives her some Miles Davis albums, takes her to see all of Chaplin's films again, introduces her to Ravi Shankar, Dire Straits, Marianne Faithfull, and Gérard Grisey.

He's completing a Ph.D. about international economics, she's studying to be a librarian, she doesn't have much spare time. But he does—he seems to have all the time in the world.

He's courting her.

ONE EVENING—it's all getting too much for her, she doesn't know what to think—she invites him up to her place. They drink jasmine tea in her studio, she stretched out on the bed, he sitting by the desk, which is piled high with all the books she should be reading instead of frittering her time away. They talk for hours and, when she gets up to show it's time for him to go, he stands up too and takes his jacket from the back of the chair. The corridor in her room is so narrow that, to open the door, she has to press herself against him as he follows her. She feels the hardness of his penis, rising up beneath the cloth, in the small of her back. He doesn't move when she turns around abruptly, as though burned, and looks questioningly into his eyes—he simply lowers his eyelids, which are almost mauve, removing momentarily the glitter of his stare from her questioning eyes, then, very softly, she can just hear: yes.

IN ARABIC, Amal means "hope." It's a girl's name, but none other would better match his oriental softness, his dark delicate skin, his long eyelashes. When she tries to annoy him, to hurt him—as she soon does, because his calm tenderness exasperates her—he writes to her. His letter is entirely made up of quotations from Lao-tzu and Zen philosophy:

"Sitting peacefully, without doing anything, spring comes and the grass grows on its own."

"He who acts will fail. Everything escapes from the man who busies himself. The Sage refrains from acting and does not fail."

"Let the prey and its shadow pass by—sit down."

"The perfect Tao presents no difficulty, except that it refrains from choice."

THAT YEAR, as chance would have it, she lives opposite Roland Barthes, whom she worships and whose *Lover's Discourse: Fragments* she knows by heart (she broke up with a man after he called R.B. a Right Bugger). When she sees him come home tired, drained, she knows only too well that this Not-Wanting-to-Grab business is an act, an inaccessible ideal, or else a device that is far too cunning for people like them. Amal abandons himself to her with a force that subjugates and wearies her. He's the perfect man, perfection made man. But she wants to choose, what she wants is to choose and be chosen in the same gesture, at the same time. She wants to grab the prey without giving up on the shadow, to trap the shadow without abandoning the prey, to love, O lord, and be loved without seeing you so calm.

He goes to New York. She's going to join him there once she's taken her English-language exam. They're going to live together, discover the world, be free and as one in the wonderful life he promises her. "Will I have time to write?" she asks.

When, a few weeks after his departure, she tells him that she's given her hand to another man, he tells her that she's made a mistake, but luckily enough she still has one hand left, and he'd like to feel its caress once more. She feels grateful to him for the repressed jealousy that nevertheless hovers above his calm letter, she also feels grateful to him for not rushing back, not regretting the freedom he gave her, and which she exploited by taking another man.

YEARS LATER, while staying in Morocco, she goes to see his father, who has a shop in the old town. He's extremely aged, but recognizes the tall blond woman his son introduced him to so long ago, and to whom he gave some men's shirts, men's scarves, the whole shop if she wanted. He gives her some tea, asks for news of her family, if she has any children and how many. She shivers as she returns his questions—how's Amal?

Amal is still living in New York, he's married to a Brazilian girl, they don't have any children, not yet, he manages a big publishing house over there, "yes, he's a big man now," his father says (there's a hint of revenge in his voice), "a very big man." "Only figuratively speaking, I suppose," she replies—she remembers his slim body, trained in the martial arts, skilled at evasive action, his softness—"only big figuratively speaking?" But he doesn't seem to understand and repeats proudly: "Yes, a very big, big man." She's sitting peacefully, holding her glass of tea—winter comes and the grass dies.

Alone with Him

WHY DO I never speak about my mother? Oh . . . you've noticed.

Well, it's because I am my mother. I'm within her, in a sense, I've always been on the inside. I know everything about her, I understand her from within, so what do you expect me to say? A daughter is always within a woman.

But it's different with a father—a man. He's next to me, and I'm next to him, there's a distance, a difference, an unbridgeable gap between us, that's why I talk about him, to fill that space, to draw nearer. But it's apparently unbridgeable, it's an abyss. I speak about it in order to evaluate it, perhaps even to fall into it.

I know that you're adopting the role of the father: you say nothing and when you do make a pronouncement, I remember it. You're in the father's role, different, or perhaps indifferent, who can tell?

But I'm not your daughter.

And don't want to be.

WHAT I WANT is to be espoused. For the other's shape, his body, his sex, his entire person, to wrap itself as closely as possible around me, as near as we can get, with as much as love can do.

"Getting married" is dumb, it's meaningless. You marry like you marry colors: put them together, make a good match. Be in agreement, harmonize nicely. Marriage means being two.

No, what I want is espousal—I want to be on the inside, and for the other to be inside me (some "in and out," as they say, when I think of it now, the expression is perfectly appropriate. With my husband, I did a bit of the old in and out—inside and outside him so that he could espouse me).

The man in me. Have the man in me. Be in the man. With no visible limit. No limit at all.

I WANT to be espoused. Totally. I want to be espoused to perfection.

The Husband

HE WAS SUPPOSED to be back by midnight, and it's past one o'clock. She locks the large interior bolt—the one he can't open with his keys—and, sobbing, writes him an elaborately phrased letter of farewell inspired by Laclos and Barbey d'Aurevilly: she's had enough of his old lovers and occasional infidelities, she doesn't want to share the empire, not her, she loves him, she wants it all, everything or nothing, she'd rather have nothing than *almost* everything. He'll find the note on the landing when he comes back, if he ever does—but she's sure he will come back, and that he's going to regret this evening, she's certain of that, too.

And come back he does, at ten past two, bounding up the stairs of their seventeenth-century apartment building, where they've lived since getting married three months ago—it's said that d'Artagnan lived there, but this biographical detail, assuming that it's true, is now starting to irritate her (it's all for him and herself now). With a deal of satisfaction she hears him unfold the letter then try to open the door with every key on his ring, then knock on it softly, scratch, shove, grumble, whisper, beg—gradually, her heart loses its bitter resentment, but this time she doesn't relent, she lets him start to wax virtuous again about that time on the train. Suddenly, the door she is listening behind shudders under a violent shock, then another, and another—you can already see light coming through the warped frame, the handle and lock explode, she pushes back the bolt just at the moment when the husband bursts bodily into the flat like in a detective film. Without a word, she leaps onto him, grabs his keys, and, unable to push him back out and beyond the doormat over which he's bracing himself, lashes out blindly at him while he tries to seize her forearms. She hits him where she can, her eyes closed, the landing light has gone out, she can't see a thing, a viscous liquid is oozing over her hands, blood, it's blood, she must have got him with one of his keys, he's wounded, he's going to die, it's the end, it's over, serves him right, he had it coming.

She's in the bathroom, he's sitting on the edge of the tub, she's gingerly dressing his shoulder with a strip of sticking plaster—the key was a bit rusty, hope and pray he doesn't catch tetanus. He grabs her hands and pulls her toward him, she smells the scent of his perspiration and closes her eyes—there was a cow on the tracks, the train was stuck there for hours and there was no way to contact her . . . What? Yes, honestly. The cow's dead.

They make love all night, stopping only to eat and roar with laughter, he tells the same story ten times over, putting on a country bumpkin accent—zo, me lady, waz this 'ere beastee yourz?—he might be lying, but now he's back in her arms and she doesn't care—her musketeer is so handsome.

"I REALLY DON'T understand it," the landlady says when she comes around. "Smashing a beautiful door like that—it was a real work of art, it was, a masterpiece of the carpenter's craft—and then to not steal anything. Because nothing's been stolen, isn't that right?"

They're standing quietly, hand in hand, on the doormat, peering with dismay at d'Artagnan's demolished door. It's love, she's sure of it, mad love, they're madly in love.

The Husband

THE HUSBAND WAS born in Étretat. That's where he takes her whenever they have a day off, or just a few hours, where they return from the distant land where soon they will be exiled. The place suits him like a rakish moustache: the husband is in fact just such a blend of gentleman thief and athletic boatman, according to his mood, he modulates between Arsène Lupin and Guy de Maupassant, monocle and sailor's smock, British humor and Norman fury, honor among thieves and the crest of the wave. This is what initially attracts her: even though he constantly brings her back to where he was born, she just cannot place him in this tiny spot, like a pebble on the shore.

The husband loves women. He always wonders what they look like undressed. He dreams of them.

As for her, he loves her, she's his lady, his spouse, his wedded wife, he forces himself to be faithful to her as promised, his love for her gives him that strength.

And what a sacrifice it is! A hecatomb! Isn't she a goddess, then?

The husband plays a number of sports on a regular basis. He has an ascetic's application. He loves suppleness, accuracy, and strength. He runs, jumps, leaps, bends his knees, straightens his arms, surges up. His body is consecrated to a sort of eternal onward lunge, a race against time and death.

The husband dresses tastefully. She often thinks that he looks like one of those deceptively nonchalant actors going up the steps at the Cannes Film Festival, providing the world with an image of utter happiness. "Gatsby," she sometimes calls him. "The Great Gatsby."

The husband collects old cars, a dream of liberty, luxury, and speed. He swears that he's never used them to pick up women, that that would be too easy, that he wants to be the sole object of a woman's desire, even if she isn't the sole object for him. In private, he likes to compare them: this one's a slow starter, but then she's a real little mover; this one purrs with pleasure; while this one here doesn't live up to her promises; and this one is really hard to turn on.

The husband loves the theater—the organization of space, the creation of illusions, to be the master of a true yet unreal world. He paces around, he creates, he escapes. He can't be placed.

HE'S A MAN who plays—a child playing stage right, by the French windows, a body bathed in sunlight. *It's better to play at life than live it*, this would be his motto. *But playing at it is also living it.*

The Shadow

SOMETIMES, spotting a workman on a building site, his chest bare, sweating, forearm wiping his brow, his jeans hugging his hips and thighs,

Sometimes, driving past beautifully shiny limousines driven by vigorous men whose sunglasses form a sort of mask,

Sometimes, seeing an actor's shoulders or eyes on the screen, in a close-up that makes you feel you could kiss him,

Sometimes, reading a book, panting under his ardent labors as he searches for her mouth,

she's seized by a brief, shameful desire for them, even though she knows they are just phantoms glimpsed in a haunted stretch of the night, showing off their fleeting powers before dawn.

But, when man displays his illusory strength, he sometimes satisfies her with all he is: an appearance—an apparition.

The Writer

SHE'S READ all of his books, she knows him through his work. People say—and he says too—that he "loves women," a magic expression to linger over for a moment (for a woman, it's always pleasant to read a book by a man who loves her, it's as though he was thinking of her). She desires him, she'd like to meet him, whenever she reads him, she wants him desperately, he turns into his own character, he exists, he lives, neither paper nor ink can stop that. She is, of course, amazed that words can create the desire to make love, but that's how it is: she cries when Jean Valjean lays out Cosette's tiny garments on the bed, she laughs when the reader of the *Medical Encyclopedia* develops every illness in the book except housemaid's knee, and when the writer watches women passing by in the street, she wants him. It's already quite something if words can provoke violent emotions, and feelings such as tenderness and pity; but you have to experience it to believe that they can affect us physically, get into our guts, make us sob, laugh, desire.

Alone with Him

MARTIN EDEN BECAUSE he kills himself, Frédéric Moreau because he doesn't dare, Gatsby because he's alone, Amalric because he relies on the softness of his hands, the sailor from Gibraltar because he gives desire the name of an island, Mesa because he endures love, Tadzio because he lets himself be looked at, Aschenbach because he dies of it, Julien Sorel because he chooses a time for action, Lady Chatterley's lover because she comes with him, Gilliatt because he keeps quiet, Romeo because he loves enough to die for it, Félix de Vandenesse because he loses control, Antiochus because he confesses (I have been silent these five years, Madame, and shall be longer), Fabrice because he renounces worldly things, Old Goriot because he adores his daughters, Vronsky because Anna kills herself for him, Des Grieux because he goes to the end of the world, Marcel because he's jealous, Adolphe because he stays, Colonel Chabert because he vanishes, Don Juan because you'd like to be on the list, Aurélien because Bérénice writes to him: "Nothing distracts me from you," Valmont because he falls in love, Monsieur de Nemour because he accepts, Lancelot because he's handsome, Solal because he knows it's impossible.

Alone with Him

WHAT CAME TO pass, what passed by—was it quite simply time, time bearing down on the upsurge of desire, covering everything with lime-scale or rust, blocking love's spring?

I don't know.

Why is it impossible?

I don't know.

WE LEFT FOR Africa. It was a sultry town by the sea, one of those cities where you feel alone in the crowd. But the French school was nice, the weather good, we were happy—I don't know what else to say, it was like years spent honeymooning—happy people have no tales to tell. We went to the pool after lessons, a huge seawater swimming pool where you could hear the massive ocean waves rolling in—my husband did endless miles of the crawl, probably enough to go around the world. In the evening, we went around to the cinemas in the various neighborhoods, hand in hand, we watched in delight the most unbelievable trash! On our days off, we read detective stories, sometimes over fifteen a week, while eating the best strawberry tarts I've ever tasted.

He loved me, I'm sure of it—I know that he'd have died for me. He was the kind of man who's capable of dying for love.

As for me, I was always afraid he'd die. I remember one day when he was two hours late, I sat down on the steps in front of our house and, while listening for the sound of his car, I tried to get used to the idea that someone was going to come along to inform me, someone was going to come and tell me that it was all over (there were no telephones in the houses over there)—at that moment, a taxi drove up, I recognized the diesel engine of those old blue Dauphines, the driver rang at the gate, and I opened it. "The police sent me to fetch you, Madame . . ." I said: "Yes, I know, I'm coming." When the taxi dropped me off I saw that the corpse was in fine shape and negotiating with an apologetic policeman on a motorbike—everyone was waiting for me so I could pay the baksheesh. But, in the end, we didn't pay, my husband bamboozled the lot of them, he even quoted Shakespeare to those delighted gendarmes, who gave him back his driver's license and forgot about the 145 k.p.h. he'd been caught doing along the coast road.

I loved that miracle about him, the way he played out his life. His existence was like a film being improvised and shot at the same time, a permanent movie. When swimming he was Johnny Weissmuller, when driving a car Errol Flynn, when kissing passionately Rhett Butler, when sad Gary Cooper in *A Farewell to Arms*. What's more, I've never laughed so much in my life as I did with him, he was all of the Marx Brothers rolled into one, putting on any number of accents, disguises, and faces.

I don't know why I'm talking in the past, as though he were dead. I suppose it's because it's over, because he doesn't make me laugh anymore.

No other man was more vivacious than him—vivacious and vibrant, vibrant . . . what am I saying? He was a man! He was men, all men, I'd married everyman, every man in my life.

It lasted a long time, a very long time when I stop and think about it; it's probably because we put on plays, he was able to go on directing and starring in our play. He was admired, people listened to him, we formed what is called a "lovely couple." "They're a lovely couple," that's what people used to say.

We loved each other, I think—we loved each of us in the other, in the mirror that beauty held up to us, in a kaleidoscope with its spangles of a multiple existence.

BUT SOMETIMES, every so often, I have to admit that I saw him differently. I came across something I wrote at the time, when I was trying my hand at a first novel (still in the drawer). When I read it over, I was surprised to discover that, even though it had been drafted ten years ago, I could have written it yesterday. I reworked it, there were a few factual details that needed changing—it was a different period then, in some ways. It ends with these words, which freeze all hope stone cold: "He's a dead man."

YOU SEE, sometimes I wonder if it isn't the man, rather than love, that dies.

The Husband

THE HUSBAND is a man out of time. In his wallet, he keeps a photograph of his father taken in the 1950s, in which can be seen an elegant man with his legs crossed, one arm rested nonchalantly on the armrest of an easy chair, which looks as if it's been taken from the lounge of a transatlantic steamer. He's wearing a herringbone jacket and shiny leather shoes. He's a foreman on the docks, but who would believe it?

The husband came to a stop there, at a time when he can barely have been born and while his father still had that imposing bearing that he was soon to lose on becoming old, sick, and obese. The husband came to rest there, on this fixed image that always gives him the pose to adopt, even in midmovement, and the way to react. He likes tweeds, English cigarettes, jazz, expensive shoes, Ella Fitzgerald, Miles Davis, *The Great Gatsby*, tea, Gary Cooper, Ava Gardner, tennis, ocean liners, old Rolexes, the crawl, and, especially, he adores the cars that were driven along the streets of that period, and more than anything the most beautiful of them, Triumphs, Aston Martins, and Jaguars, he loves those wonderful cars that his father couldn't afford.

The husband is a man out of time, from his father's time. The future may have made a few incursions into that black-and-white world—he also likes the Beatles, Fellini films, Philip Roth novels, and liberated women—but when time freezes for him, everything comes to a halt and the only light left is the one being shed on the ancient image of a past existence. He detests rap, hamburgers, tags, piercings, vulgarity, motorways, trainers, advertising, concrete promenades, women who smoke in the street, druggies, sociology, Mercedes, techno music, T-shirts, stock options, Virginie Despentes, Disneyland, communication technology, game shows, television, people's stupidity, and, above all, he hates what's happened to language—"No," he keeps telling his daughters. "You do not say 'it's cool' or 'it's awesome.' You just don't."—the way people speak meaninglessly, that language made of words that has lost its words.

SHE CAN UNDERSTAND that, she shares his nostalgia. But sometimes, as the years go by, she cracks (she plays some Cheb Khaled full blast), and when the husband comes over all sad and melts away into the photo of his still young and handsome father, sitting cross-legged in a leather easy chair, fleetingly she merges the two of them together: "He's a dead man."

The Actor

AFTER A WHILE, they get bored in Africa. She starts writing a novel, and her husband puts on plays. He directs as he lives, bringing together words and images, gestures and texts. He starts up a company and spends entire nights in the gleam of the red curtains. This is where he excels, where a truth springs up that she so admires. In the evening, when she isn't writing, she plays at obeying him, body and soul.

The actors come and go with the seasons, travel, and friendships. Only one remains for years, rooted to the stage by the depression that invades him as soon as he leaves it, which he chases away on his days off with drink and sordid affairs. The actor is the dark side of the husband, something like the doomed part of his soul. The theater, booze, prostitutes, and drugs: he couldn't put up with anything except paradise—that of art and that of artifice, which is so close to hell, pierced with bright flames.

She acts with him, he becomes the chosen actor, the male lead, the dear friend, they act together. He kneels down in front of her:

"Ah, my dear Lisette, what do I hear? Your words contain a flame that has pierced me. I adore you. I respect you. All rank, birth, and fortune vanish before a soul such as yours . . . my hand and my heart belong to you."

"In truth, would it not serve you right if I took them? I would have to be generous indeed to conceal the pleasure that they give me. And do you think all this can last?"

"You love me then?"

"No, I do not—but if you ask once more, then too bad for you!"

HE TURNS his back to her, she sees his whole frame quiver, as his hand grasps the cardboard rail.

"I know you do not love me."

"What a surprise indeed! Here is what I have just learned: I am the one you would have loved."

He turns back around, she's never seen him look this way before.

"Then let me look at you. How bitter it is to see you here, with me. Why did I have to meet you now? It is hard to keep one's heart entire. It is hard not to be loved. It is hard to wait, to endure, to wait, to go on waiting and waiting, and here I am now at this noontide, in which one sees what is close so clearly that nothing else is visible."

THE HUSBAND DIRECTS them; they're inseparable. Every year, the plays are chosen according to which parts they will play. In the evening, they go to the bars of luxury hotels, the two of them with their felt hats, monocles, cigarette holders, or two-tone shoes, she between them, in a tight black leather skirt, her face hidden by a veil. The actor does cocaine, the husband has a single malt whiskey, and she drinks fruit juice. There have been rumors about the two men, ever since they were seen onstage bare-chested dancing the tango ("the tango is a man's dance," the actor insists), they've been nicknamed "The Bermuda Triangle." When they're together, the lights on the stage where they're acting never go out, they put the world to rights between stage left and stage right— "We should put on *Othello*," the husband says. "I'm sure you'd make a perfect Iago." "You're right," he replies. "I have a treacherous soul." They laugh.

Then the actor leaves the country, and them. He goes back to France, to a forgotten family, a wife and children. They miss him. But when she thinks about him, everything seems vague and unreal, she's full of confused impressions, as though she was remembering a performance seen long ago, she can't separate what she felt for him in her heart, what she feels when she recalls him—and him for her, for them—she can hardly make out the past. In front of her eyes there is a thick fog that conceals a moment in the wings, when suddenly you are no longer in the footlights.

The Stranger

THE STRANGER IS in front of a cinema, waiting for the ticket office to open. It's the midday showing, there are very few people. He looks at her. She lets him.

In the cinema, she takes a seat near the front, as usual. He doesn't. She forgets about him so completely that, when the lights come back on, she leaves by the emergency exit.

Later, she's waiting for a number 21 bus a hundred yards up the road. He walks along the boulevard, when he notices her he stops, he comes toward her, but not in one swoop, by degrees, with pauses, as if in some animal courtship ritual, a parade—it's verging on the ridiculous. Finally, he's standing beside her. "Did you like the . . ." he begins. "Look," she says, "I'm only in Paris for two days, so what else can it be but a brief encounter?"

He gets on the bus with her, she notices his long slender hands, a wedding ring (he's probably thinking exactly the same thing). They get off together, she goes to the Pompidou Center, he'd like to see her again. "This evening," she says. "At the Cluny."

He arrives on time but explains that he can't stay: his wife's pregnant and started crying just as he was going out. He only came to be polite, so that she wouldn't wait for him. He apologizes. She tells him not to worry.

He leaves her in front of her hotel and dashes down into the metro. She goes up into her room, sits down on her bed and cries, she cries with her arms crossed over her belly, her head leaning on her knees, she cries for ages. The light coming in the only window is like a gap in the shadows.

The next evening, she goes down to have dinner and he's there. He makes her go back into the lift, he touches her, he trembles, she closes her eyes.

His mouth, his skin, his tongue, his hands, his fingers, his hair, his arms, his legs, his buttocks, his back, his lips, his eyes, his penis, she knows it all, she knows all there is to know about his sex, except his name—she doesn't know this man's name, he remains a stranger.

THE FILM they saw together is David Lean's *Brief Encounter,* made in 1946. Nothing happens in it. It's like a dream you should wake from and never mention.

SHE MENTIONS the stranger to no one. She keeps him to herself.

Alone with Him

THE REASON I'm saying nothing is to make you say yes, that's all, I'm being quiet so that I'll be able to hear you, otherwise you'd say nothing, and I want you to speak, I want your voice to touch me, to reach me. I'm waiting for you to say yes, just like the last time I stopped speaking, after two or three minutes, you said *yes* in a quite wonderful voice, which I couldn't imitate but can certainly remember, yes like a man who loves a woman, yes as though you were coming to take me just as I am, to take me no matter how far away I am, that's what I want, I want you to say it and say it again until I believe you, until what it opens inside me stays open, yes, when you say yes like that, it has a ring of love to it, I know, I should remain silent, I'm burning my bridges, I know that, you're not going to obey, of course you aren't, on the contrary, you're going to watch your tongue and never say it again, I know that, you're going to abandon me in my silence, in my sorrow, in death, even though, yes, you could say it again, quite simply, yes.

The Lover

THE LOVER WORKS with her, that's where they meet. She's an assistant librarian at the school where her husband teaches English and the lover teaches German.

It's abroad, in an Arab country where it's forbidden to look at men or speak to them; where any relationship at once takes on the terrible weight of the stifling air; it's a country where women don't breathe.

She didn't learn German when she was at school, she didn't want to, because of the sound of jackboots. She was born later, but that changes nothing, it's still the enemy's language. Since then, she's read Goethe, Hölderlin, and Hofmannstahl, she knows how beautiful it is, even in translation—beautiful but terribly alien: a difficult, hostile tongue. A language that is totally foreign.

Even though the lover is French, he incarnates this language she doesn't understand. He becomes the personification of that hermetic tongue: beautiful but alien. At school, she overhears him talking with an assistant from Stuttgart, she hears him laugh, joke, explain something in German. All of her senses are focused on the mystery of this man. She understands nothing.

Around her, on the streets, people converse in Arabic. She knows more Arabic words than she does German ones, but nothing that's worth saying; desire has been smothered in the egg and hatches only in song, in Umm Kulthum's voice or in *raï*—otherwise, it's dead, or nearly, a language of undressed timber, a brutal tongue.

SHE WANTS to learn German to conquer the lover.

ONE DAY, she writes to him—in French, of course. She writes these words on a plain sheet of paper: "I would like to talk to you."

The Lover

WILL HE CALL? What time? Can we see each other? When? For
how long? Where? In which hotel? Does he love his wife? Does he
make love to her? Does he love me? Does this dress suit me? Is
he going to like it? Does he prefer blondes? Am I too fat? Does he
find me attractive? More attractive than his wife? More intelligent?
A better lover? Do they do the same as us when they make love (if
they make love)? Does he say the same things to her? Does he love
her? Does he love her more than me? Does he love me?

Is he going to leave his wife? Am I going to leave my husband?
Should I? Wouldn't that be a mistake? Is he jealous of my husband? Shouldn't I make him jealous, send him mad with jealousy,
push him to the limit? Does his wife have her suspicions? Is he
afraid she'll find out? Is he afraid my husband will discover what's
going on? Is he afraid? Is he a coward? Are all men cowards? Are
all men bastards? Is it just for sex? Shouldn't I split up with him?

What time is it? Has he been held up somewhere? Has he had
an accident? Will he come? Is it over? Does this mean it's over?
Doesn't he stop work at five on Tuesdays? Is that his car outside
the gate? Has he gone to a show with his wife? Could I speak to
him? Could we have five minutes to ourselves? Do other people
have their suspicions? Is he lying to me? Has he had enough of

me? Has he had other affairs before me? How many? Has he been in love? Really? When? Was it a long time ago? Does he still think about it? Will our affair last? Is he thinking about me? Does he miss me? Does he know that I love him? Am I wrong to tell him and show him that I do? Shouldn't I instead be more distant and reserved? Does he know I'm waiting for him to call? Is he going to call? When? What time? Why doesn't he call? What will I say to him if he does? Should I stick to everyday chat and avoid any questions or signs of anxiety? Does he love me? Does he really love me?

Alone with Him

I LIKE IT when you say: "Let's leave it at that." It's odd, because it means the opposite, it means: time for you to leave. When you say "let's leave it at that," it's to make me leave. You say it nicely enough, in a friendly tone, but say it you still do, you decide that it's time for me to leave, that it's over.

Men have problems keeping women close to them, apparently it's caused by a common physiological phenomenon: after making love you have a so-called "withdrawn" period, a time of insensitivity during which nothing must be asked of you—withdrawn indeed, and withdrawn in fact, from the body lying next to yours, from the woman touching you, perhaps even from the very idea of having to go on—to speak, start all over again, to acknowledge this tie, however slight it may be, that both binds and alienates you. Are you thinking? Are you afraid? What's going on inside, what do you feel? Depression, weariness, disgust? Disgust with yourself, disgust with your partner? Shame? Shame at being that extinguished, withdrawable, withdrawn body? Shame at being there, as naked and helpless as on the day you were born, beside a woman who you fear will ask you, is already asking you, has probably never stopped asking you, to give her what you cannot give, because you don't have it either, no, you don't have it, and she's asking you for it, that's why you're ashamed, isn't it, the hole you're in that she doesn't know about, so instead you prefer running away, or for her to push off, that's it, push off, scram, that's withdrawal for you, a ray of light refracted on the surface of separation, now only departure is possible, a breaking up when roads fork and there's nothing left in common but the past—no future. Yet still I love, I love it when you say "let's leave it at that." I can remember someone, a man, who used to get up, go to the window, open the curtains, and then, as though his decision were based on what he could see in the street, would promptly claim that he had to go—he used to say: "I have to leave now," meanwhile concealing his withdrawn penis in a fold of the curtain, but what had really withdrawn was his entire body, dying to leave, to vanish, it was his entire self that suddenly wanted to be off, out of there, cancel everything, I deny every word of it—that's right, scram.

WHAT'S BASICALLY HUMILIATING about all of this is that you all go, or else ask us to go, afterward—even just after. What's humiliating, I mean, what pushes our faces down into the earth for a foretaste of death, is that you leave us with nothing of yourselves, at least, not voluntarily (sperm and sweat, of course, memories of you, but if you could, you'd take the lot away with you). You withdraw like a murderer withdraws a confession made in a moment of weakness—you said nothing, did nothing, you weren't even there. By leaving, you deny everything, and that witness who claims she saw you, that woman who testified that you were there, well, she must have dreamed it, because it wasn't you. It wasn't you. How sad, in fact, is there a sadder end than denial? *Animalia triste*, as they say in Latin.

Which is why I like "let's leave it at that." Because it means "let's separate," while implying that there's something left to return to, a trace of an appointment, even if it's missed, a means to reconcile the desire to know and the will to forget, the desire to admit and the will to deny, to unite in you both entry and withdrawal, attraction and pleasure, here and there, the past and the future, the leap and the fall—because what's left, that residue left between the sexes that everything opposes, what's left stands up to death, to sadness, to men's sad fates, maybe it's love, what people call love. And when the lover leaves, love is left behind. So, let's leave it at that for today, leave it, leave it for a time, leave this moment to last a little longer.

ALL RIGHT, I'm going, don't worry, I'm going.

The Husband

THE HUSBAND KNOWS about the lover. She doesn't know how he knows, but know he definitely does. He knows that she's got a lover, and he knows who it is.

He says, oh well, that's the way it goes, these things happen, there's nothing anyone can do about it, it doesn't really matter. He too has had affairs in the six years they've been married—two, or three maybe, yes three in fact—but never anything of any importance, which is why she never noticed, isn't it? He has always been discreet, plus none of them lasted very long, and sometimes he felt disgusted with himself, horrified, and sorry for her, and it's generally because the woman wanted it, because she wanted him. He can't say no, he's touched by women's desire, even when they're old, even when they're ugly, especially then in fact, maybe he acts like this so that she will never be in danger, will never have any serious rivals, so in the end it was nothing very important—no, it wasn't with Marie, why do you think it was her? No, I've always said we never, no, I wouldn't lie to you, not about her. Why should I tell you who it was, what does that matter? What? The cow? It was true, I swear to you, there really was a cow on the tracks—not even affairs in fact, you can't really call them that, more like flings, extremely brief, things like that happen, he's not going to make a scene, it happens to everyone, it can happen even when you're in love, like they're in love, it's desire, OK, right, let's forget it, it's water under the bridge, let's drop the subject.

She tells him no, she can't just forget like that, how can you forget the present, how can you forget what you're experiencing, for her, it's the present, it's now, it's real, it isn't over, not for her, it's only just started—barely two months of sneaky encounters, she hasn't had enough time, she wants to know him, to get to know him better, she wants to see him more often, to continue, it's her future, so let's not drop the subject.

He tells her that she's a real little bitch, he can still hear her quoting Sacha Guitry's wife's famous rejoinder as if it were her own: "I'd never cheat on my husband, because I couldn't stand being married to a cuckold," very funny, wasn't it, how they all laughed, and he believed her, what an idiot he was, he'd worshipped her like an angel, an idol, does she even realize that, he'd made an angel of her, in his eyes she'd always been different, pure, innocent, and now where was he? a pathetic cuckold, that's what, cuckolded to the core, and betrayed by the very person he'd placed so far above the others, above all that shit, all that slime, no, really, what an absolute fucking idiot I am.

She says: "Why mention shit, why do you always drag everything down, why . . ."

He tells her there's no point play-acting anymore, he's seen right through her little angel routine—a right slut, that's what she is, all she thinks about is getting her pants off at the first opportunity—and what an opportunity, just look at him, that creep can't weigh more than a hundred pounds with his boots on, a runt, a maggot—this is surely the hardest part of it all to swallow, I mean just look at him, have you ever taken a real long look, for Christ's sake, the sort of guy who must be a really lousy lay, the sort of jerk who comes faster than Christmas.

She says nothing.

He yells: "Whore!"

She closes the window.

He yells: "Oh! So you don't want everyone to know that you're a whore, a slut who spreads her legs for the first creep she sets her eyes on. But that's what you are, there's no other word for you: a whore. What do you take me for, for Christ's sake? I mean, just take a look at me! I'm thirty-five, not an ounce overweight, a lung capacity of four hundred cubic inches, I can screw the night away no problem, what more can you ask for? And I don't know if you haven't noticed, but, around here, all I'd have to do is whistle and dozens of them would come running, blue eyes are a rarity around here, so when it comes to the ladies, I could pick up who I want to, when I want, girls prettier than you, younger than you, real nymphs, virgins, just look at you with your fat ass, I mean what the hell were you thinking of, go on, get out of here, go back to your poison dwarf, go and get fucked by that little piece of shit, go and suck his dick, you bitch, but just watch out, that's all, be careful, because when I'm gone, I'm really going to be gone, so just think it over, you might regret it when you've had enough of shagging lousy little shits."

"Not that lousy," she murmurs, frowning at such untoward language.

He doesn't reply . . . in both hands, he picks up the large glass table that stands between them and hurls it against the wall, where it smashes into a thousand tinkling shards. He goes over to her and slaps her around the face so hard she feels her head buzzing on the edge of oblivion, she raises her arms, he grabs the neck of her dress and shakes her violently, his eyes staring madly, his mouth foaming—with a loud rip, the fabric tears completely apart, a dress she's just bought, which suited her so well, she manages to grab his wrists, stop, she yells, stop. He then breaks a vase and the arm of a chair before abruptly slumping down onto his knees: "I

love you," he says. "Can't you see that I love you?"—then he
cries.

She stays still, standing over him by the fireplace. She squeezes
her hands so tightly that, as she will soon find out, her wedding
ring has lost its circular shape forever. Finally, she lays her hands
on his shoulders, which are quaking with sobs, and she stares out
of the window, into the distance, stiff and motionless in her dangling dress.

COSTUMES NOT by Donald Cardwell.

The Lover

YOU'RE BEAUTIFUL. I desired you the moment I first saw you. You've got wonderful eyes. Never before have I felt so loved in love. You're beautiful. I love it when you come. I want you. You've got lovely breasts. I love you. I've had a row with my wife. That dress really suits you. You're beautiful. I'm thinking of leaving my wife. Your book's wonderful, I adore what you write about love, were you thinking about me? I dreamed of you all last night. It's no good with my wife anymore, in fact it never has been any good. I want to take you in my arms. I'll be expecting you at five. My wife's jealous. Your husband's looking suspicious. I couldn't make it, my wife suspects something, doesn't your husband? I don't know if I can. You're really beautiful. I don't love you enough to wreck everything. My wife's depressed. Is that a new perfume? I love your mouth, I adore your mouth. My wife keeps asking me questions. I can't, next week maybe. What did you do last weekend? You're looking down. What's up? You've got wonderful eyes. You make me come—I can't stop thinking about you. This will have to stop, it's utterly impossible, your husband's going to murder us, he's completely nuts. We're being foolhardy, this isn't reasonable, it just isn't possible. Let me think, listen to me, understand me, I mean you do agree that he's crazy. You should leave him.

Come into my arms. No, not tomorrow, I'm taking my wife to the
beach. It's true, I do feel great with you, but we should stop seeing
each other for a while. It was you who picked me up. I never promised you a thing. It's impossible. I don't feel like it. Not now. No,
not tomorrow. Look, this must stop. It's over—it isn't easy for me
to say it, but it's better this way. It's over. I never really loved you,
I just fancied you, which isn't the same thing at all. I don't love
you, stop, that's enough, I want us to stop, it disgusts me, I'm
going. I want to see you again, I've been thinking about you these
past two months, I want you, I want us to make love again, I can
get the keys to a flat on Thursday, I know you love me, I love you,
you know that I've always loved you, I've loved you from the moment I first saw you, even before I got your letter, I dream of you
every night, tell me you love me, you're beautiful, you've got lovely
eyes, you've got lovely breasts, my wife's gone to France for three
weeks, you're looking down, what's up? Come into my arms.

Alone with Him

I'M WRITING a book about men, a novel about the men in my life—that's what I say when I'm asked. Subject: Man.

But the truth, the real truth, is that I'm writing to men, for men, for them. Writing is the thread that will join us. By writing, I'm attracting their attention. Subject: Me. I'm full of men, that's the subject.

If we really always do write for someone, then this much is clear: I'm writing for you.

I haven't finished yet, far from it, but I've already found two possible epigraphs, with completely different tones, to use at the beginning. I'm going to show them to my editor later today.

This one, by Marivaux—I'm quoting from memory (the Marquise has recently been widowed):

THE MARQUISE: I tell you, I've lost everything!

LISETTE: Everything! You scare me: have all men died?

THE MARQUISE: What do I care if some are left?

LISETTE: Oh, Madame, what are you saying? May heaven guard them! Do not disdain our resources!

I LIKE the idea of resources, the man as source. Literally, in the eighteenth century, a resource was "something to improve an awkward or unpleasant situation." And being alone is certainly an unpleasant situation. But then, the man suddenly appears, he drops in from nowhere and brings happiness with him. *Some day my prince will come*, how often I sang that song when I was little . . .

Or else, there's this other excerpt, which is less lighthearted and extraordinarily erotic, by none other than Paul Claudel. Amalric is talking to Ysé—Amalric, as godless flesh, soulless love:

> I have pleasant hands
> You know perfectly well that nowhere else than with me will
>   you find
> The strength that you need and that I am the Man.

I am the man. Isn't that marvelous? A man who comes over to you and says: I am the man.

You'd then need the strength to stare back at him and say: I am the woman.

Nothing else—just that, in these very words, just as I've framed it: I am the woman.

BUT IT ISN'T that easy, is it? Me Tarzan you Jane. Difficult, isn't it? If we could name each other, if we were able to introduce ourselves in the clarity of our sexes, in the sureness of our being, in the proclamation of that double truth—Me and the Other, the Other and Me—we wouldn't write, there would be no stories, no subject, no object.

I WOULDN'T WRITE if you were the man. I'd probably just live.

The Editor

WHAT IS IT about these periodic meetings with the editor that so inspires silence? What is it, from year to year, from book to book, that adds such gravity to the words we exchange, so that personal communication becomes difficult, if not impossible? What's missing in this immured relationship, what's required for her to believe in it?

After each meeting, she feels as if she's been slipped back onto the shelf of a glazed bookcase, whose door closes at once—she may never have left the row from which he reached out to take her, maybe he spoke to her from behind that transparent screen and everything sounds muffled; what could have been radiant and sunlit has been dimmed.

She doesn't mind being treated like a book, she can accept it, but not just any sort of book. She wants to be one that you turn back to constantly, that you know by heart, whose every word you can remember, but still without solving its inexhaustible enigma—the favorite book, the one that's never really filed away, that remains at hand, at arm's reach, accessible, a bedside book. So, instead of hoping vainly that a union between book and reader will occur during social chatter, she says nothing, she shuts up (when you have nothing to say, you say nothing).

There's a particular kind of pain in such silences—or in the chitchat that conceals or furnishes them. It's extremely reminiscent of the jealous moods in childhood when, as one among sisters, you wallowed in the despair of never being the favorite.

"For me, each author is unique," the editor declares in an interview, thus compassionately standing in as the perfect father for whom each of his children has an equal place in his heart.

Unique, she repeats to herself pensively.

What persistent hunger there is in such a daily round of finishing one book then opening another one.

Unique she might be. But she's not the only one.

Alone with Him

THERE ARE forbidden men, men you find forbidding. I sometimes wonder if that awesome distance expresses the true nature of love—to be both here and there, *on one side and the other*—or else its utter impossibility—how can you love from a distance, without touching anything in the other person?

The point of desire you have to cross to reach the other shore, the point of desire you have to *pass over*, even if it means dying.

The First Love

FOR ALMOST TEN YEARS, she sees no more of her first love, they lose touch completely.

One day (she's just moved to Africa with her husband), she receives a letter in a blue envelope, postmarked Lyons. It's from him.

He got her address in Africa by calling her sister, Claude, who also gave him her new last name, because she's now a married woman. He can't understand or come to terms with the fact that she's married. Why did she do that? He's single. He lives alone. How about meeting up again?

When he opens the door at the top of the staircase in an old building in the third arrondissement, the first thing she notices is his short-cropped red hair, which now looks lighter than it used to be and flecked with white. He's put on a bit of weight, but she recognizes him and, when he gives her a hug, she breathes in his skin, like a recovered memory.

He tells her his news, what's happened during all those years.

He passed the entrance exam to the Polytechnique—she knows that, the last time they ran into each other was at the ball there, and they pretended not to notice each other. If she remembers correctly, he wasn't that keen on going to a school with such strong military traditions, he was a pacifist, wasn't he? . . . —That's right, but you know, when your father's a general . . .

He now works for a big oil company, but he's trying to get a new job, he's going for interviews, so far no luck, he just doesn't feel at home in his present position, everyone gets promoted ahead of him, his salary's not up to his qualifications and experience, he's thinking of hiring a lawyer.

AND THEN THERE'S something else, a secret that, incredibly enough, was kept for three decades and that he has only just been told: he's Jewish. His father was a soldier in Algeria, from where he brought back and married the austere young brunette who used to smile at her when she went to see Michel—she remembers her opening the door on its latch, as though terrified. "Your mother's Jewish and you never knew that?"

No, he didn't. His father had sworn the entire family to secrecy and even now he still refuses to talk about it—what did it matter if he was Jewish or not? He didn't want to be circumcised, did he? His mother had kept quiet.

The first love is sitting there overwhelmed, no, I mean, can you just imagine it, an entire people is wiped out and my father just says "Who cares?" She takes his hand. Look, Michel . . . He closes his eyes as she strokes it, but pain is racking his face. On the shelf behind them, his father is unsmilingly displaying his golden stripes, soldierly shoulders, and virile features.

He takes her to dinner in a kosher restaurant. "And so, you got married?"

He's had some flings, of course, as well as some longer relationships, but always with women who aren't free and who won't leave for him, there was one in particular whom he really loved, she had children, things didn't work out, and—"this will make you laugh"—her name was Camille.

All he has now are one-night stands with girls he picks up here and there, he goes to parties, he never uses condoms, he's for mutual trust, and anyway . . .

Back at his flat, he takes her in his arms. She wants him, she remembers Sundays when she was sixteen, she remembers the plans for the future they made in bed. But he doesn't kiss her, he whispers to her that they don't have to make love, they could just lie together, spend the night in each other's arms, she could sleep there, with him.

TOWARD THE END, long ago, they didn't have sex for several months, she slept with others, but they were still in love, still touched each other tenderly, fraternally. She remembers their chaste slumbers when she slept with him, pregnant by another, and his friendly face in the waiting room, where he'd sat motionlessly for hours while she was having her abortion because he wanted to be there to give her a ride home.

They are back at precisely that moment in time, in virginal tenderness, half happy, half sad: that's where they are in the doorway of his bedroom, that moment, ten years ago, when they separated, embracing, feeling like death. That's where they are, despite all the years: at the departure point. It's as if they'd never split up.

SHE DOESN'T STAY, she runs away, she makes something up. "Wait," he calls after her when she's already going down the stairs. "Wait." He gets a camera and takes two Polaroids of her, with her back half-turned, which she doesn't wait to see developed.

SITTING IN the metro, she breathes in the odor of her first love between her fingers. In the tunnel, darkness dotted with light shoots past. She thinks of how some men feel that they do not have the position they deserve in the world and how this makes them suffer, as if someone inspired by tyrannical hostility had pinned them down in this pathetic weakness ever since they were children so that now, in the middle of brilliant careers, with lovely personalities, this fault line abruptly reappears in the form of some otherwise inexplicable failure.

The Correspondent

THEY MET at a symposium and have written to each other ever since. He's married with three children. He asks her if she'll become his sister.

She likes getting his letters, at the beginning it's a pleasure to open a letter, read it, get to know a man through his sentences, their rhythm, their parentheses—his letters are like a mind breathing, the respiration of intelligence.

She provokes him, tells him what she thinks about men, what she thinks of men.

He writes that he loves her. He writes what she wants to read, tells her what she wants to hear: he loves her, that's what.

FROM THAT MOMENT ON, everything falls through—their correspondence no longer corresponds to the situation. It's not that she doesn't love him—she was tempted to reply "me too," "so do I," "I love you too," but these words rang as hollow as a plaster cast, as flat and dull as the pattern on a frieze that continues indefinitely along the edge of a plinth or ceiling. "I love you," "Me too"—as if they were the same, not different, him in the north, her in the south, corresponding: can such words be written down

162 | CAMILLE LAURENS

without becoming drowned out in the text, do they travel well, can they survive the journey?

She sometimes bitterly regrets losing the correspondent. She should have been more patient, less headstrong, she should have looked at the good points of a distance whose lumps of stucco she smashed to pieces, instead of considering their beauty and power. But she has no patience, she isn't one for seducing the invisible man; for her, absence does not make the heart grow fonder, she rejects such exasperated desire, an impossible intercourse that the flourishes of language cannot really conceal. "I love you," "me too": plaster and junk. No relationship.

THAT'S WHY SHE invariably sabotages any exchange of letters with a man she finds attractive, the only correspondence she keeps up for long periods without wrecking is with women, because in this case distance is a virtue. And yet, she knows that bodies often reply even more poorly than letters to the infinite hope of desire. But she'd still rather be burned alive in the nakedness of a presence than constantly put off the only possible response, the response that shows up all their differences by magnifying them (as you are not a correspondent, I'll make a point of telling you), the only possible response is in physical terms: here I am.

The Brother

SHE, OF COURSE, has no brother. She sometimes thinks it's better this way, that she wouldn't have been very good at being a man's sister, making his body abstract, giving up physical contact. But this is probably because she doesn't have a brother: she has not been in a position of loving a man on a daily basis without also desiring him, she did not go through that trial by fire in her childhood—the father doesn't count, nor does André, they are on another time scale—and this is presumably why it makes her suffer so much more today; she isn't used to such torment: to be close to a man, near enough for him to give his lifeblood, his soul, his days and hours—someone consanguine, a coeval, what the Church calls "your neighbor"—and to have to chase away any idea of a caress.

On the bus, she frequently bumps into a spotty youth dressed in a priest's robes. When she sits next to him, he smiles at her and always says: "Good morning, sister." Apart from the fact that she's old enough to be his mother (not superior, his real mother), she hates this family they are trying to impose on her. "All men are brothers," yes, of course, she remembers reading that somewhere. But what reassures her after a moment's thought on the bus—and she smiles to herself—is that if all men are brothers, all women aren't their sisters.

———

HE WOULD HAVE taken her to the cinema, and to his parties, he would have introduced her to his friends, told her about the books he was reading, he might have watched over her, spied on her, bored her, cramped her style, he would have envied, mocked, hated, admired, served, betrayed, left, followed, forgotten, and re-discovered her.

But would he have loved her?

How do brothers love their sisters? What is this love that has the same name as another?

SHE DOESN'T REGRET not having a brother, and no one can fill in for him. "Love your neighbor as yourself," *"mon semblable mon frère,"* "we few, we happy few, we band of brothers," "sphere-born harmonious sisters"—she just can't swallow all that literature that eliminates the irreducible otherness at work in our species.

She has no brother anywhere in the world, and it's just as well. So she knows only one kind of love: instead of reassuring famil-iarity, she far prefers the disturbingly unknown. She loves her neighbor as another.

Alone with Him

ABEL WAITS—what an odd name you have. A brother's name, a religious brother, I mean—there can't be that many mothers who call their sons Cain . . . And quite feminine, too, you can just hear it in its tonality, the sound of "belle," whereas in Cain there is nothing but masculine aggression. In fact, there's nothing particularly surprising about that: the gentler brother, the girl-brother, gets beaten to death by the virile Cain.

But I suppose you don't have any brothers . . .

ABEL WAITS—the good brother who waits, watches, and waits. I've seen others like him in the countries where I've lived—thousands of brothers watching, waiting, with their mothers reproducing again and again more of the same wretched, baneful copies. In such places, a brother stands for the death of woman.

But, in the end, is it that different here? The style is different, luckily enough. But don't you think that this fraternal sympathy, this sympathetic fraternity between men and women, is also killing us? Doesn't it destroy what we are, one by one, melting and mingling us into a shapeless mass of humanity, of Mankind? "Till death do us join!"

We are all Men, we are all Women?

We are all brothers, we are all sisters?

Everyone is a man, is a woman, is a brother, is a sister, and also the same.

Doesn't grammar show up this kind of absurdity for what it is? If everyone is singular, how to finish the sentence and still have it make sense?

I'M NOT AGAINST pity, charity, humanitarian work—that's not the point.

I'm against the attempt to set up in our society, by means of a network of tacit conventions and regulations, a situation that can in fact be obtained only via its diametrical extreme, what no brother or comrade ever receives or gives in his inane desire for family or familiar unity: the profound sensation of Not-Me, knowledge of the Other.

I SUPPOSE you've noticed that there's a man called Amand who lives in your building—Amand de Shade. Abel waits and watches while Amand, he who is chosen for love, remains in the shade—we've got two different types of man here, apparently.

There's no sex in your name, or at least no admission of there being any. With a name like that, you could have become a priest.

Or a psychoanalyst. Someone who specializes in marriage counseling.

Everyone's brother.

Everyone's, except mine.

Jesus

CHRIST IS rather a good-looking man. She understands the women who take him for their husband. If she goes into all of the churches she comes across, it is for him, Jesus.

Jesus has a fine athletic body, a body made for struggles, dancing, love—Jesus has a man's body, a beautiful naked body, which is constantly being thrust before us to remind us of things spiritual, of flesh that is dead or destined to die, of vanity.

But there's blood beating somewhere in an artery, in the hollow of his neck, or did she just dream it?

IS IT A CORPSE you see in church, or a suffering, abandoned body, given over to spears and stares? Sometimes she forgets both possibilities, when the wounds have been taken away and the almost smiling face distances it from martyrdom, all she admires then is the almost naked male body, stretched out in front of her like a swimmer reclining on the grass after a dip, arms crossed beneath the heavens, breathless, deathlike, turning his head toward the warmth coming down through the clouds; in the stained-glass window, all she can see are his bulging muscles after an effort relaxing below his skin, which still has the whiteness of late spring.

Yes, sometimes, when she goes to contemplate Jesus in churches, she forgets that he's dead, she forgets this as completely and mysteriously as we forget, when listening to a Bach mass, that God doesn't exist.

Christ is a handsome man who is suffering and seems to be offering himself to us. But is he a man who could be made happy? She doesn't think so. This explains why her worship remains discreet and distant. Jesus might possess every possible masculine attribute—muscles, beard, strength, and courage, as well as a male organ modestly concealed by some sort of diaper, even when he is no longer a baby. It's a man, the son of Man. But he has no woman, no desire for a woman, you can see at once that he will never take you in his arms, neither before or after crucifixion, and, if by some miracle he did, his embrace would be icy and nothing would arise to make happiness last. He has no woman, no family—this son who is a father, this son who will never be a father, this god of love who is never in love. She doesn't believe it. He gave his life for her, did he? For her, not to her. He never gave her a thing, apart from a tormented body to contemplate that is out of reach and cold-blooded—*noli me tangere*.

WHEREVER SHE GOES, she always ducks into churches, she goes to see Christ, Christ's body. She recognizes the power it exerts over blind hearts and seeing eyes. She commiserates with those poor women who adore him with no return, the lost souls who imagine he died for them, because, when you look beyond his beauty and suffering, all you see is a form of absence: the body seen on display everywhere does not display love. She just can't believe anyone could possibly feel good on that breast or in those arms. This isn't the chest to lay your head on, or these aren't the shoulders where you could rest your soul, but vanity, just vanity.

The Lover, the Husband

AFTER SPLITTING UP with the lover, she cries for two years. This is not an image meant to conjure up sorrow, she really cries, every day—and not always in the silence of her bedroom or when alone: she cries in the restaurant where her husband takes her to cheer her up, she keeps on crying—tears fall into her plate giving everything the salt taste of sea air.

The husband could murder her. When the eye specialist asks her how her retina became unstuck, she says that it was an accident. He operates with a laser and advises her not to wear contact lenses anymore because, he says, her eyes are too dry.

THE LOVER DOESN'T answer her letters, and when she grabs his arm in a doorway at school, he pulls himself free without a word. She cries, she remembers everything he said, what he used to say: *I love you*, and also *I don't love you*. Her tears form a curtain of rain that attempts to smear both of these sentences into one landscape.

She can't understand how such a thing is possible: *I love you*, then *I don't love you* from the same mouth, then in the same silence.

I love you.

I don't love you.

———

THE LOVER IS not a man of words. He's been struck dumb. She writes him love letters, she wants to understand—where's the truth? She says: "I would like to talk to you."

The lover doesn't reply, he keeps his word to himself.

She writes him love letters, she tells him she's unhappy. The lover doesn't reply: he's not responsible. There's no reply to the letters she sends or the love she offers—she doesn't speak his language.

One afternoon, there is a tea party in the staff room. She cried all last night on the backseat of the car—"go away," the husband yelled, "go away or I'll strangle you"—she saw the sun come up, dawn gradually turning the rear window pink—I love you, I don't love you. They serve scalding mint tea in steaming glasses, the tray is passed around. The husband picks up one with the tips of his fingers and throws it into the lover's face—"this is your cup of tea, I guess," he says in English then leaves without looking at her; she's petrified, a statue of salt. The lover sits bent over, looking stung, dabbing at the tea on his cheeks with a tissue, as if wiping tears.

SHE CRIES FOR two years, she even cries after he has moved on. Then she gets pregnant with her first child—the one who will die, but she doesn't know that yet. Only then does she forget the lover, the irresponsible lover. Her mind gives up crossing the distance that separates love from disgust and the lover from her. I love you, I don't love you: the soul reconciles itself to this unsolvable puzzle, the body accepts that there is no answer to it, any more than there is to the greatest mystery of all: I am alive, and then I am dead.

———

IN NOVELISTIC TERMS, the scene should have a different ending, years later, recalling patience and oblivion, the length of time, its convoy of coaches, hermetically compartmentalizing the most contradictory words and mutually exclusive events. Nothing fits, no two things go together, each moment is discrete, no word is anyone's bond: one morning, she has a fit of hysterical laughter, while her husband is pouring hot water into her younger daughter's feeding bottle, she laughs, she just can't stop laughing, she laughs till she cries and, between bursts of laughter, she says to her flabbergasted husband: "Do you remember the mint tea party?"

The Son

SHE HAD a son. He died. When people ask her if she has any children, her reply is the same as her mother's: "I have two daughters." At the beginning, she used to mention her son by name. Then she stopped doing so, people didn't really understand. She stopped, she never refers to him.

He's every woman's absent child—absent, whether they have six or seven, or don't have any at all. It's an absence for the women who don't want children, who'd never have kids, not for all the tea in China, for those who dream of babies, those who have babies, those who want babies. It's an absence for women who have abortions, who don't keep their child, who abandon it, refuse it, and for those who adopt, who choose, who hope. It's an absence for pregnant women, sterile women, women who can't have any more, old women.

It's the child who's here-but-not-here, it comes and goes, back and forth like a shuttle. You get used to its absence. For her, it's a son. For others, a daughter. But it exists. All women have a child.

It's an absence for men, too. This child, this son, this image of themselves, this future of themselves—blood, face, name—it's an absence for all of them, even for those who take precautions, who withdraw in time, who emerge covered, who don't give a damn, who are too busy right now, who say no, who hate screaming kids, tears, bonds, family attachments, who just can't stand children— it's an absence for all men, even child-killers. All men are fathers.

THIS IS just to make you understand: she has two daughters she loves passionately. But there's also the child who's absent, and whom will be forever absent from her arms, he's hers too. She has a son. It's him.

The Husband

HE TRAVELED all day but gets there too late: the child has already been born, and the child is already dead. He goes into the room where she's expecting him, where all she's expecting now is him, she stretches out her arms, he goes to her, he's here, she's holding living flesh and blood.

WHEN THEY MADE love months before—on the brink of the abyss—they mingled their mouths, fingers, bellies, they mixed their faces and limbs, and their orgasms were screaming out for a miracle: they were making a baby.

PLEASURE WAS inconceivable. Death wasn't. Death was conceived.

THEY SAY THAT we are all haunted by two unknown moments: our origin and our end—twinned moments, like bodies embracing, man and woman, pleasure and death. She remembers the cliché to which they once said yes: for better or worse. Everything works in

pairs, she with her husband and him with her, his twin, they go together.

WHEN, in the morgue, the husband puts his arm around her while
she rocks her dead baby, she knows that she will never be closer to
another man than she is to him, never, even if she had a thousand
of them, distance has suddenly been reduced to zero, and their
bodies are buried one in the other as though in earth or in darkness.

The Doctor

THE DOCTOR DECLARES that all is well, there's no cause for concern, no treatment is necessary: his eyes avoid her stare, her fear, her trust. Two hours later, the child dies; he doesn't come and tell her, a nurse does: the child (not *your* child, but *the* child, you know, *the* child, the one that didn't have time to be *yours*), the child is dead.

The doctor was a brilliant student in the same town as her. He's four years younger than her, when she took her leaving certificate, he must have just been starting high school, but probably at Saint Jean's and not at the state school—she thinks he looks Catholic, yes, definitely Catholic: the son is destined to die and the mother must accept this, *mater dolorosa*. He hasn't learned what to do when the child dies, what you should say to the father and mother, it wasn't taught at school, so he has no idea. Nor does he improvise, he's a rigorous, well-organized, methodical doctor, like his father before him in the very same clinic.

SHE GOES to see him after the funeral, she makes an appointment at his surgery, she goes to see him, she can't leave it there, without a word, without understanding.

But he has nothing to say, not a word. If she wants the file, then she'll have to apply to one of his colleagues—patients have no direct access to their medical records. He fiddles with an engraved metal guillotine.

Patients.

She isn't a patient. She's impatient.

WHEN HE STANDS UP to bring the appointment to an end, an image flashes before her eyes: with the back of her hand, she's sweeping everything except the probe off his desk, she's pressing him down on the wooden surface and raping him, brutally, just like that, why? why? to make him make another one, that's all, to remake what he's unmade, to make amends, that's why, because she wants her child, she quite simply wants him to give it back to her, he's fair-haired and pale, he probably has children like him, just like the child the color of whose eyes she will never know.

SHE LEAVES. Her husband is waiting outside, she didn't want him to come in with her, he would have lost his patience. She cries in his arms, she cries with shame, she's half dead.

AT FIRST, this image obsesses her, this shameful, unspeakable, atrocious fantasy: she can see herself above him, straddling him violently and the earth that they're digging up, that they're sowing. Then she gets a clearer picture of the scene and what is taking place: in that monstrous wrestling match, she's penetrating him, she's on top, brutally brandishing the weapon, man's strength, shoving in a spade that opens a hole of red clay in him, in that wild struggle, she's the one who's unmaking, destroying, devastating. No, there are no amends to be made, no, this man cannot save anything, give anything, offer anything, so she kills him, right there, she kills him, she kills him, she kills him.

The Grandfather.
The Father. The Son

SHE'S PREGNANT for the first time, there's less than a month to go before the birth, it's a boy. She goes shopping with her mother, they get in the car, they talk about the baby clothes they've just bought. Her mother must be carrying on some sort of covert conversation because, like an underground stream breaking through to the surface, she suddenly says:

"In my day, it was really hard being a girl. I mean, I did love my father, he always spoiled me, I was daddy's darling little girl; but, actually, when I think about it now, he got in my way. He always got in my way. For instance, I was very good at athletics, I beat everyone in the one hundred meters, I could have been a champion, like Colette Besson; I was even selected for the French championships, did you know that? I was really good—but obviously that would mean going to Paris, and my father wouldn't let me. He said it wasn't right, that girls shouldn't show their legs, that the only reason men went to stadiums was to look at girls wearing shorts. He was a sportsman himself, he was mad about rugby, but he just wouldn't let me go.

"And then, I also hold my marriage against him. You see, I was in love with my cousin Georges—no, you don't know who he is, even I've never seen him since, that's over forty years back now—he was a distant cousin on my mother's side, I wonder what became of him, sometimes I feel like writing to him, I know he lives in Lille, but I'd better not, he might look awful now, men change so much, get flabby, lose their hair, I'm lucky to have André, they often don't make any effort, you know what I mean?—I mean, they make no effort compared to us. Anyway, in those days he was wonderful, I was really in love with him—my first love. But he'd left school early, he was a traveling salesman. So my father wouldn't accept him.

"He was hard, when it came down to it.

"MY FATHER MEANT everything to me, but I didn't mean everything to him.

"MEN ARE FREER, don't you think? So it's good to have a son, it's better. Even though things are different now. All the same, I'd have liked to have one, and your father wanted one so much, he must be pleased he's going to have a grandson, mustn't he? He wanted one so badly. Maybe things would have worked out better then, maybe your father would have loved me if we'd had a son."

Alone with Him

IT'S INCREDIBLE, I was just on the point of telling you something about men and me, I had an idea, which might not have been
very important, but it mattered to me, and suddenly, *pfft!* it's gone,
I just can't remember it.

I'm trying, I really am, it's not far, but I can't reach it, blanking
like this is so irritating—it escapes me.

IT WAS ABOUT the difference between men and me, what that
makes me feel, even when I feel good and there's no conflict going
on with any of them, or even when I'm feeling strong, how, despite everything I experience our difference physically: that's what
I wanted to tell you about.

Because, as a matter of fact, I often feel as if I were a man—I
mean: I don't feel feminine in the classic sense of the term, I feel
more virile, in fact. That may be because I have the trappings of
their power: a profession, I write, I'm published, I'm independent.
I often act like them, even act like a caricature of them—this disdain for mere flirting, a will to take the initiative, to take the first
step is their prerogative, at least, traditionally it is.

—————

I WAS ONCE told some gossip about me. Apparently, when everyone at work heard that I was pregnant—so, almost ten years ago now—one of my colleagues, a man I'd known for years, and who I got along with well, exclaimed: "Oh, so she's got ovaries has she?"

Which was quite funny, really.

BUT THAT'S NOT what I was going to say, that much I'm sure about. Oh, it's on the tip of my tongue but I just can't find it.

NO, IT'S GONE, it's lost for good.

IT'S LIKE a black hole.

The Psychiatrist

SHE GOES TO see him because she's lost her child—her first child—no one can tell her why exactly, but he died at birth. She buried him across the sea, in France, then came back here to this completely foreign land. In this country in Africa, thousands of children die every day, so obviously not many tears are shed over them—what's more, everyone believes in God, and it's God who decides.

So it's easy to see why there's only one psychiatrist in the town. She has no choice, so goes to him.

The waiting room is packed—at least thirty people, sitting on the floor, standing with their heads leaning back against the wall, or slumped on sofas. She remains in the entrance, by the door, a man tells her to cover her hair. The women wail and wring their hands, their eyes are crazy with an insanity that looks like resentment, they're out to get you. Why? You don't know.

She's shown in before all the others, the secretary comes and fetches her, because she's white, because she phoned for an appointment, what's more, she isn't mad, she can see that these people are there to wait, or at least they're used to it, for them it's just one more day spent waiting in a life spent waiting, it passes the time, and practically makes their suffering pass, too, they have nothing better to do.

The psychiatrist studied for two years in Reims. She doesn't know it. Champagne, he says. Yes, of course she knows champagne. He asks where she was born, she tells him. So what brings her here, to what does he owe the, what can he do for her?

She tells him. For the first time since it happened, she remains unmoved by her tale, like stone, like a bad actress in a lousy role. He says yes, of course, he understands—but, when it comes down to it, it isn't that serious, she'll just have to get over it, and she will, he'll help her; they have the same treatments here as in New York or Paris, so not to worry.

He doesn't tell her that she'll have other ones, he tells her that there's more to a woman's life than just children. He tells her about his time in France, he goes over to a bookcase and removes a bound volume—his thesis, with a letter of congratulations from Henri Ey, he shows it to her, she reads it.

Henri Ey is a great psychiatrist, but he supposes she knows that.

WHEN SHE'S ABOUT to leave with her prescription, he takes her in his arms, in an apparently almost paternal way, without going for her mouth or anything, and he holds her, she can feel his lips in her hair. She remembers her father who, when getting divorced, used to round off the occasional letters he sent her with "my fatherly kisses." It's a bit like that. But if she wanted, it could be different, all she has to do is want. While keeping hold of her, he shifts slightly away, it's up to her now. She can see that he's fed up with it all, with the people in the waiting room, with loonies and hysterics—one of them is now wailing and screaming—he's had it up to here, the same routine day in and out, he can't go on, he needs a change, a new life, to be elsewhere, or still here but with her, she looks normal enough, and she's blond.

She hesitates for a moment, she wonders whether to give him that pleasure. No, she won't. There are too many people waiting for him, she doesn't feel up to making him forget them all, neither the desire nor the strength to forget so many. At the chemist's shop downstairs, she hands in the prescription. They have everything she needs.

Alone with Him

IT WAS a rough period for me. I was utterly alone: neither a mother nor a mistress, I had neither a child nor a lover; I couldn't even choose between being a mother or a whore, all the roles were being played by others—other women pushing their prams in the park or brushing past my husband in the street.

That year—for nearly two years, in fact, from the death of my son to the birth of my daughter—those years were a strange, unique experience for me: suddenly, there were no more men. Not one. Nor was I a woman anymore, but instead a grave, a black hole into which everything had collapsed. The earth was empty.

Before that time, I used to look at men, I used to spend most of my time looking at them. Not many realized it, few noticed. It was a secret—I loved them in secret. My husband has always been more flagrant, more obviously on the lookout, more keen—he tried to conceal it, but I could see his desire as clearly as my face in the mirror.

Then, abruptly, the earth emptied. Even my husband practically vanished from view, all I had left was a chopped-up body reduced to its sexual functions, scraps of a body to darn onto what was left of mine in an attempt to form an entire one, to remake a man, a son.

I was crazy. Crazy with pain and hope: to make a man.

———

WHAT DID my husband turn into during those two years? A penis and sperm, a sperm donor, nothing more: I needed him to make a man. He slipped into an anonymous pit of oblivion.

For two years, the only man in the world was the one I was going to make.

For two years, the only desire in the world was the desire for a child.

IS CREATING MAN women's triumph? Is carrying a male sex in their bellies an incredible challenge for them?

A GIRL WAS born. With her, men returned with their eyes, arms, and faces—and, with them, the humility of my desire: I learned what I should have known, it isn't women who decide if it will be a man, it isn't women who make men.

The Husband

THE HUSBAND LOVES women. He needs women like she used to need men, long ago, when they still existed for her. He aches for them. She can't blame him, because it was this very need that she loved in him at first sight, that she recognized in him. She loves that love, even if it surpasses her, because by so doing, it also includes her.

The husband isn't slow off the mark—she's often noticed that—all he needs is a crumb, anything will do, he would drown in a tear. She can sometimes see it coming before he does, he's going to drown again, she knows it as well as her shadow, as well as her reflection.

At the beginning, she's jealous (she dreamed of being his one and only crumb). Then she stops, even though she still experiences a suffering that typifies disasters, like when people die side by side absorbed in their own deaths; their destiny might be the same, but all communication is gone. Sometimes, when things are bad (the husband is sometimes rejected), she doesn't have time to be truly compassionate—she'd like to say: look at me, I'm the same, just look, I'm like you. "You wouldn't understand," he says, with his head in his hands. "You just wouldn't."

She knows. He's the one that doesn't know how she has delved into this very same mystery, has tracked the same prey.

She knows. He's the one that doesn't know it just isn't worth it, that there's no point.

DURING THE TWO YEARS of the earth's emptiness, the husband is merely desire in suffering, an abandoned body looking for bodies of abandon. He never thinks of anything else, he even admits it, he yells it out, anyway she's not listening to him, he needs women. Is it a disease, as it was with men like Simenon and Chaplin, or so they say? He wonders about that. According to him, the pull of sex is like a mental illness: just look at what lunatics in asylums do all day. Sex is insane when it separates instead of unites, and man is expelled into the madness of solitude.

For two years, madness gains ground. They're both mad: her for wanting only one, him for wanting them all.

SHE USED to be jealous. But not since she held her dead child in her arms, that body she'd expected and desired. She has no religious faith but when she grows angry against her infidel, compassion returns, forgiveness for those poor offenses so redolent of innocence. She doesn't believe in the soul, that much is sure, but she does pity the body.

The Passerby

SHE'S EIGHT MONTHS PREGNANT and walking slowly along
the pavement alone. The passerby stops as he overtakes her, then
slows his step to keep pace with her. What a lovely day it's been,
it's hot, how delightfully hot! She goes as far as the traffic lights,
freezes on the edge of the curb, chin up, staring at the little man
who's taking his time about turning green. What a lovely blouse,
with those flowers on it, it really suits her, what are they exactly—
tulips or roses? She speeds up as she crosses, the passerby keeps up
with her, their arms touch, she pulls aside. Phew! What heat! He's
dying for a Coca-Cola, now there's an idea, he'll buy her a drink,
he knows a nice quiet café just nearby, how does that sound?

She suddenly stops in the middle of the pavement, facing a
palm tree, and, without looking at him, tells him to go away and
leave her alone.

Then, before she's set off again, he rams a sharp index finger
right into her belly, while spitting out his question: "And I suppose
you got this one on solar energy, did you?"

The Forgotten Man

IT'S WHEN reading *Le Monde* that she remembers the forgotten man: there's little doubt about it, the first and last names are rare enough, and, when she knew him, he was finishing his studies to practice the profession mentioned in the obituary.

SHE MEETS HIM through a friend, his cousin. He has classic good looks that appeal to everyone and he hates the fact that all women think so. When he can, he avoids spending any time with them; in general, he thinks they're stupid, mindless, hysterical, and—he doesn't mean her, of course—obviously inferior to men.

When she gets to know him a little better, he tells her that he's only ever been in love once, years ago, many many years ago—how old must he have been? Eight.

He'd like to see that little girl again, but he hasn't managed to trace her, she must have changed names, that's the problem with girls, they change and we lose them.

ONE EVENING, she's sitting next to him on the settee, she lifts her hand and gently touches his shoulder. He melts straight into her, arms first, he dives in and undresses her mechanically, without kissing her, he hugs her and rubs himself against her nakedness, she feels the harsh woolen cloth on her skin, that clothed body twitching in anxious spasms, and impotent tics. Then, a quarter of an hour later, when she smiles at him sweetly (it doesn't matter), he stands up, takes his coat, and says: "No, it doesn't matter. It's just that I'm not used to . . . I mean, making love with whores. To be honest, making love with whores just doesn't turn me on."

WHEN HIS NAME in the obituary rings a bell, he'd already been long forgotten. The article recalls how "that day, he took his own life." Three years earlier, to the very day, she gave birth to her daughter—the same date, a shared anniversary. She thinks of the hatred men sometimes have for women, of the struggle that opposes them and that only a few, perhaps, from either side can survive (you see them in the street, with their evil stares and twisted mouths). She also wonders how he did it, if he killed himself by hanging, poison, drowning—in fact, she can just see him throwing himself into the Seine that March day; with a degree of admiration, she pictures him succeeding perfectly where most women fail and thus scoring a final victory over them.

Alone with Him

YESTERDAY, I read an interview with a biologist—a geneticist, I suppose. I was on the train, I thought about it for quite some time . . . He claims that only women ever really want to have children, during his career he's never met a single man who's been truly haunted by this desire, and, for example, when it comes to artificial insemination or medically assisted reproduction, men always remain out of the frame, withdrawn, they're only there to make their wives happy, and a pathetic desire to run away is written all over their faces.

Do you really believe that? Don't you think that it's in fact quite the opposite? That men want to have babies with their women? That they live out an eternal dream of fecundity and fecundation? Making love and making babies are just about the same thing, logically speaking—practically the same collocation. The same goes with desire: to want a man, to want a woman, to want a child; see how shocking, but also revealing, grammar can be sometimes?

I've often felt this very thing with my husband, but also with strangers: that they wanted me for more than just myself, that I'd been put into perspective.

So, I reckon that if a man leaves his partner for a younger woman (which is what my husband did when he met me, for example), then it isn't because her breasts are sagging or her butt is like this or like that. No, not at all. Men leave women when they can't have any more children.

The Traveler

THE GRAY-HAIRED, rather corpulent man sitting across the central aisle during the long hours of a train journey and who, when a little girl's sleepy voice can be heard singing "Frère Jacques" from the end of the carriage, with a flash of desire and tenderness of a sort she has never seen before in a lover or a husband, smiles at her.

The Husband

ONE DAY, he comes home from the school for underprivileged teenagers, where he's been teaching English since their return to France, it's March, she's on maternity leave, she's not working and living in dread of the future birth—a girl, she knows it's another daughter. He hangs his coat up on the hook, "hey, what's that you've got on your back? Come here . . ." He goes over to her. His pale woolen jacket is dotted with blue and black stains—it's ink, they're ink blots. He removes it, takes a long disbelieving look at it, then, head in his hands, he slumps down onto the couch. His pupils have discovered this simple, silent way to amuse themselves: when he writes on the blackboard, or walks between the desks to help them out individually, they flick ink from their fountain pens onto his back, like darts.

The next day, he brings the subject up in class, he talks about humiliation, disdain, tolerance, and mutual respect, he says that you should never, ever, defile another person.

When he gets back home, he doesn't even think to check his jacket. She's the first to see the stains. She doesn't dare tell him, her heart is crushed, she feels that this is a trial from which neither of them will escape alive.

The husband absolutely refuses to compromise, he declares war without shifting an inch, this is a matter of dignity: no, he won't change the way he dresses, even if his elegance does make them hate him, he won't change a thing—that's it, *he will not change,* if he did, it would mean accepting a negation of himself, surrendering to an intolerance set on dragging him down to neutrality, making him wear a uniform, merging in with the masses, and just look at them! So no, he won't wear a T-shirt and jeans instead of the suits and ties he buys in London, he'll remain true to himself whatever the cost ("of the laundry bills?" she asks, trying hard to laugh), this is the best lesson he can give them, the only thing he really wants to teach, when it comes down to it: how to remain yourself in a crowd.

Every day, for weeks, he gets ink on his clothes.

He no longer walks among the desks, he doesn't write on the blackboard much, he stands facing them, he faces up to them.

At home, he says little, barely looks at their first daughter, who's still a baby, forgets about the coming birth. He remains lying on his back for hours, gritting his teeth, fists clenched. He's alone.

She tells him to stop, to take some days off. She asks him to tell the headmaster and his colleagues, she begs him to write a report to the Office of Education.

He doesn't. He says that everyone else in the school thinks the same way as the children, his colleagues—"in their uniform casual look," he sneers—think that he's a pretentious snob, and vain with it. For days, T. S. Eliot's *The Hollow Men* lies open on his desk on the same page:

> This is the way the world ends
> This is the way the world ends
> This is the way the world ends
> Not with a bang but a whimper

She writes on his behalf to the inspector of schools, she signs a letter of distress, she sends out a Mayday for him, she says he's fragile, they've lost a child, and things can't go on like this.

Three weeks later, the addressee replies—the letter is postmarked Paris.

Dear Colleague,

You have a caring wife who is worried about your professional situation. I think that you should take a long hard look at your teaching practice. This is a new and rather delicate post, to which you must adapt. It is a good thing if the most highly qualified teachers, such as you, communicate their knowledge to more underprivileged children—this guarantees democracy in our education system, an equal opportunity for young people to succeed, and represents an extremely enriching experience for you. Furthermore, I find it hard to believe that you can look on the dark side of life for too long in the country of Paul Valéry and Georges Brassens.

Yours truly, . . .

Two days later, the husband spins around suddenly and catches a pupil with his arm raised, pen aimed at him. He walks over to him and punches him in the stomach; the pupil fights back and, among the other pupils who are now on their feet, they start pummeling each other between the desks, screaming, fighting to the death.

The next day, the husband puts on his most beautiful tie to go and teach. His opponent is absent. There's no ink on his pale jacket that day, or on subsequent days. Far away, in the heights, the sun is shining on the cemetery by the sea.

We are the hollow men
We are the stuffed men . . .

Those who have crossed
With direct eyes, to death's other Kingdom
Remember us—if at all—not as lost
Violent souls, but only
As the hollow men
The stuffed men.

The Stronger Sex

Passing faces, what indecisive clause
Do you write up but then always remove
And must what you try to say and improve
Be ever doomed to beginning again?

SHE LOOKS at men. Of course, she doesn't look at them in quite the same way as men look at women, because she supposes that only the most attractive ones draw their eyes, while all she does is try to spy out what makes them men; while they contemplate beauty, she peers into a mystery, while they scrutinize each passing face and figure as a singular fleeting presence, she tries to uncover a single, universal meaning—a secret, their secret.

THERE'S THE MAN who, on a plane, works on his laptop one row in front of her, on the other side of the aisle. He's young and already balding, wears horn-rimmed spectacles, and, just now, has read all of the *Libération* newspaper except for the book pages. Maybe he's a writer who prefers not to know what the others are doing. He types on his keyboard quite rapidly, stops to think from time to time, consults his handwritten notes, pinches the top of his nose between his thumb and index finger, leans his head back against the seat, his eyes half closed, breathes deeply with a profound sigh, then starts typing again. When the plane starts its descent, a typewritten page flutters out from a file and falls onto the floor; she picks it up and hands it back to him, while swiftly taking in the first line: "Production Costs as of 1st March 1998: Quarterly Prices on the Shallot Market."

THERE'S THE MAN who, on a different flight, talks about the stock market with his colleagues and refuses to turn off his cell phone because he's expecting an important call from his broker. Then, when the air hostess offers him a basket full of sweets, he rotates his forefinger for a long time in concentric circles above it, before diving down onto an orange sweetie, and suddenly, incredibly, he's six years old.

THERE'S THE HANDSOME young man, very blond and pale, wearing a blue sweater, who's walking toward her on Boulevard Saint-Michel, clutching against his chest something that looks from a distance like a drawing board, he then abruptly drops to his knees at her feet, and, while the other passersby move to one side, he brandishes in his outstretched hands a notice containing these words written in block capitals: I'M HUNGRY.

THERE'S THE MAN talking to another man in a restaurant. He has an intelligent face, bright eyes, and beautiful hands. He explains that there's lots of money to be made in this field—but she hasn't caught which—"loadsamoney," he adds, "piles of it," "I'll be rolling in it." Then, when his companion finally stops ingurgitating his pizza long enough to be able to confirm his interest with

202 | CAMILLE LAURENS

an enthusiastic "great!," the first man pauses for a moment, then says: "If you want, I'll sell you the idea."

THERE'S THE MAN who goes out for a box of matches and is never seen again.

THERE'S THE MAN who beat up and disfigured a woman in an underground car park: "I opened her jacket and blouse, I pulled off her trousers and panties, I felt her breasts, stomach, and vagina. I was going to shag her, but the sight of those bruises on her face stopped me from getting it up," he said.

THERE'S THE MAN who raped a young girl who was in a coma after a suicide attempt. It could only have been the male night nurse, or else her father who had watched over her agony. It was the father.

THERE'S THE MAN who, in order to stop the customs officials who are trying to inspect the boat in which he is an illegal immigrant, throws all of the children overboard one by one.

THERE'S THE MAN who picked up a twenty-year-old girl and stabbed her twenty times over before cutting off her head and sending it to his ex-girlfriend: "When I'd killed her, I felt happy."

THERE'S THE MAN who runs over a little girl who then stays attached to his back bumper, so he attempts several quick stops in the hope of getting rid of her.

———————

THERE'S THE MAN who, in front of his partner, buries alive their newborn baby because, he says, his mother is very religious and would never have accepted it.

THERE'S THE MAN who practices fist-fucking with a razor blade hidden in his hand.

THERE'S THE MAN who insults, kills, tortures, massacres.

THERE'S THE MAN—there are the men. To understand them, she tries to fathom what makes them different from women. But their secret eludes her. She tries to identify what makes them men, she lingers over this point: they do things no woman would do, or else do things differently from how women would. But, regrettably, she cannot rise above this cliché: their violence, the brutal way they live, their desire to dominate; except perhaps by linking it to what deceptively seems to be its opposite: the fragile, retarded, huge children in them, which may be the true crux of their savagery—and sometimes she feels pleased that she hasn't had a son, for when attempting to find a point of balance in the space that runs between the will to win and a child's despair, a place where, acrobatically, the ideal man would be standing, she has to admit that, despite all her love, whenever she does glimpse this fluctuating point clearly—a tightrope walker's harmony between strength and weakness—and finds that someone is there, it's always a woman.

Alone with Him

MEN ARE SEPARATED from women forever.

Just listen to Couperin's music, for example, *Les Barricades Mystérieuses*. The piece lasts only about two minutes . . . it's shorter than a love song but it says it all, as clear as crystal: I try, I approach, I come, I come back, the air trembles, I say this and that, the same thing or practically, always rephrasing it, shading it, repeating it—*I love you,* maybe; but hang on, someone's stopped me, who goes there, who are you, who on earth are you?—silence falls, the mystery remains.

Man and woman: mysterious barricades. A lesson in shadows, if you can learn from the night.

The Actor

THEY DON'T SEE each other again for a long time; their phone conversations become less frequent, they seldom write. She sends him her books. When she loses her child, she gets a letter from him, she recognizes his sumptuous handwriting on the envelope, the words inside are sweet.

AFTER THEIR OWN RETURN from Africa, they organize a party and invite the entire gang from far and wide. The actor is there, they hook up, they dance, they laugh, the lighting in their memories glitters brightly.

At dawn, she's asleep in her room, everyone has gone, except those who live too far away and are staying the night. The actor lies down next to her: "I love you, I've always loved you, you know that, don't you? You know you're my angel, the most beautiful angel it's ever been my good fortune to see." He holds her face in his hands. "Always, right from the start, from the very first day, you've been my good fairy, my dream, and I know you know that, my beautiful angel." He's trying to inch his way under her nightdress, between her tense thighs, into her silent lips. "You remember the time you left me the keys to your place, when you both went away on holiday, well, I went by every day to rummage through your clothes, your panties, your perfumes, every day, my beloved angel." He pushes his body against her, she backs off, what time is it, the streetlights are still on, everything seems to be asleep, and where's her husband? "Since the very first day, you know that"—no, she has no recollection of any desire.

She pushes him away and tries to get up from the bed, where he's holding her down. "Stop," she says. "Stop it," she calls him by his first name several times, and finally manages to break free.

Then he, too, gets to his feet. "Some people have all the luck," he begins. "Don't you understand what's going on? Do you know where your Ideal Man is? The Perfect Husband? Just go and have a look in the garage: they're sucking each other off, him and her, go and see for yourself, he's licking her pussy and she's giving him a blow job, just go and look . . . That asshole screws anything in a skirt, as for me . . . Meanwhile, you're here playing Penelope! Get your revenge at least, for fuck's sake. Let's get our revenge!"

They remain motionless for a long time, staring at each other.

She walks into a ray of light.

"What is it called when the sun comes up, as it does today, and all is broken, all is wasted, and yet the air can still be breathed . . . ?"

He raises his arm toward the curtain.

"It has a beautiful name, my lady Narsès. It is called the dawn."

The lights slowly come up, brightening the scene, each sees daylight in the other. Then darkness.

Alone with Him

AT THE MOMENT, I'm trying to go out with more men; it's a bit headstrong of me, but nice too—a horizonless philandering, an aimless stroll—I'm drifting.

I read the personal columns, I meet men's eyes, I look up old friends. I'm letting men get near me.

Last weekend, I was in Orléans for a book fair. The first night, there was some confusion at the hotel where I was staying; when I got back about midnight, the night porter said: "Oh! your key's not on its hook, someone else must have taken it." I laughed and answered that, normally speaking, I was there alone and so he should thank the manager for being so thoughtful. He laughed and blushed then found the key.

The following night, after a ghastly day, I wearily recite my room number—this time the night porter asked if I'd like some tea or coffee. I accepted. When he stroked my hair, I turned around at once to get a look at his eyes. There is a science of strangers: you read their eyes—not their hands, or their words, but their eyes.

To my mind, the worst, most abject kinds of men are the ones who despise women's desire. I don't mean the men who turn down a woman because they don't find her attractive or because they love elsewhere; I'm talking about those who desire while despising the desire they provoke. Then you see in his eyes what he's seen in yours, ah, so that's what you want is it? that's what you're after—a sort of mean glint that either stabs you like a dagger or else places a mask of stone on your face, you can't smile anymore, you have no face anymore. I've seen that flash before, on several occasions, even from seriously loving lovers—that scorn for my sexuality, the fear of the wound, of what I am, even in those who love me, yes, it rushes in from afar, from way beyond love, as though hatred were simply love's flip side, its hidden features, that hatred of others that makes it what it is—and it scorns you as much as it hates itself, and its father and mother, and the world and its wife. At such moments, nothing seems slighter than the boundary between desire and the desire to kill, and nothing pulls men and women apart or draws them together more than this commonly shared fear they experience that binds them even as it separates them: the fear of murder. To wipe out the Other, hug it to bits maybe, abolish it, eliminate this desirable body, this demanding soul, get rid of this separation in death, turn our difference into nothing, crush it, stamp on it, wipe it out, yes, that's it, wipe it up with its blood. That's what I can sometimes see in their eyes. In man, murder is just close by, under his skin, panting, glinting in his eyes like desire, written all over his face. In a sense, murder is just one form of desire, it's the desire to give it to you once and for all.

When you see that in a man's eyes, you should run, obviously, you should run. Often you stay. A woman looks for the love of her life, but sometimes he's the love of her death, sometimes it comes down to the same thing.

The Single Man

THE SINGLE MAN IS good-looking fit elegant refined classy sensual dynamic tender attentive protective sincere intuitive cool generous authentic optimistic profound old-fashioned tall slim humanitarian enthusiastic attractive curious sensitive artistic down-to-earth romantic integral spontaneous free extremely free free between noon and two dominant discreet intelligent into life's rich pattern active nice cuddly a nonsmoker left-wing divorced married Jewish nonpracticing virile religious but unorthodox strict well-off postanalysis bursting with humor keen anticonformist idealistic tolerant witty relaxed distinguished well-balanced aesthetic epicurean feels good looks good good man all around.

The single man likes foreign travel.hiking the really important things in life the sea sport art cinema socializing painting music photography books children bridge skiing boating the quality of life junk shops human values the theater exhibitions large breasts high-quality relationships and nature.

The single man seeks desires would like to meet dreams of expects longs for an attractive sensual pretty voracious similar naughty tender slender sexy dominant experienced slim feminine remarkable sincere with pierced vagina voluptuous young lively ample well-proportioned seductive open-minded partner muse drop-dead

gorgeous nordic blond sweet sensitive affectionate liberated free
or slightly married get-up-and-go libertine latino rambunctious
passionate cuddly fun romantic lusty cheeky leggy curvaceous half
castes welcome wicked provocative refined top-model stunning
merry delicate loving soul mate

for a relationship that will be marvelous a great fling excep-
tional moments together absolute love close complicity erotic fun
and more multiple liaisons sincere commitment naughty weekends
away real trust lasting friendship kisses and cuddles sensual get-
togethers calm and voluptuousness playful initiation nice surprises
intense libido playing around to form steady couple tantrism moon-
lit romance during summer/winter to be defined

to share fun and frolics freedom leisure emotions laughter pleasure love passion life passionate life and happiness ideal ideally share
everything

to explore pleasure share the millennium reach to a future love
build and create discover ecstasy keep the flame burning turn our
lives into one long poem limitless love take Highway 69 life to the
full receive/give construct love avoid the routine really go for it
build a new life experience passion reach nirvana seventh heaven
ecstasy and more if compatible.

The Reader

THE READER ISN'T singular. The face he offers changes from
day to day.

The reader writes to you. He's heard you on the radio or, more
likely, seen you on television, or in a photo in a magazine, he's seen
you and he wants to write to you (he doesn't say he wants to read
you, it is clear that the reader often doesn't read). Not to beat around
the bush, his name's Bruno, he's twenty-eight, he's a student, he's
got a part-time job as a librarian (just like you, isn't that right?) to
pay for his studies, but he can't complain because his job allows
him to meet lots of people—and meeting people matters—plus
he loves being around books, he's quite passionate about being
around such volumes crammed with history—and passion matters. He knows that you're passionate, like him (he quotes one of
your sentences, but not from one of your books, from an interview
you gave to a high-circulation weekly magazine—it's clear that
circulation matters), and if you have a spare moment, he'd be only
too delighted to discuss the matter further over a drink and a
paella—he makes excellent paella because (like you) he lived abroad
for some years—travel matters—he's also passionate about travel,
discovery, and exchanges. He gives you his address, phone num-

ber, e-mail, and cell number (you must be just dying to contact him at once to exchange your impressions).

THE READER COMES to see you. He was at primary school with you on Rue Jeanne-d'Arc, you remember, don't you? He's put together a scrapbook of articles about you, which he shows you along with a class photograph, that's him, there, at the back on the right, just behind the globe.

THE READER TALKS to you, he asks for the microphone. In your previous book, you deplore the fact that the young don't read anymore, you're a librarian aren't you? In a secondary school? He used to be a teacher (but not anymore, he's been promoted) and he can assure you that his experience is radically different, that he got hoards of underprivileged teenagers lapping up Rabelais, Racine, and Corneille, you just have to know how to go about it, but, of course, not everyone has been blessed with such an ability, what's more—he then gets to his feet and everyone can see that the reader is an attractive thirty-five-year-old man (thus younger than you), well built, well dressed, well all around (a lot better than you, anyway, who rushed here after a day's work without even enough time to do your hair before getting onto the stage, sitting down behind your bottle of mineral water and bearing witness to the vitality of literature), what's more, he adds, standing, talking directly into the mike, you often speak about the sensuality of words, physical contact with them, earlier you used the word "erotic," but right now, when I look at you (he looks at you: you're wearing gray, you stained your pullover when gulping down your cup of tea at the gas station, you smell of perspiration), I'm sorry, but I just can't see anything erotic at all.

You remain composed (*I was talking about words, dickhead, the contact with words, not your smug prick*), you reply: "Sorry, if I'd known you were coming, I'd have worn my fishnet stockings." You get laughter on your side, but you swear that never ever again will you answer the reader—neither your *semblable* nor your *frère*—the enemy.

THE READER WRITES to you—he isn't used to doing things like this, in fact it's the first time, but he just can't stop himself, since reading your latest novel, he feels as though he's being propelled onward by a newly discovered need. His name's Bruno, he's twenty-five, he's a student, he recognizes himself in your male character, he's just the same, with that loving, passionate nature, he's like that, too, and he's looking for his ideal woman, who will understand him—and, oddly enough, he felt understood in your latest novel, he'd like to meet you—he's a librarian in S. but would willingly go wherever you ask, he gives you his address and phone number; if you replied, you could tell him that you already have them, that he should update his author(ess) file, because it's clearly in need of a thorough revision, but you can still congratulate him on being three years younger than when last he wrote—has he discovered the secret of eternal youth?

THE READER THANKS you. He's just read almost half your novel while standing on the pavement outside the bookshop, he casually opened it after buying it on impulse, and is now writing to you on a table in a café where he had to go and sit down, he felt so moved: thank you for this book, thank you for this deeply human moment. He signs with his first name, but gives you neither his last name nor his address, which you regret, because his way of remaining thoughtfully discreet and anonymous means, of course, that you'd like to meet him—and only him.

———————

DESPITE WHAT people say, the author never reaches out to her readers. She's sure of that. What keeps them forever distant from her is the illusion they're under, in which they think they know her, can reach her through her words; this semblance of truth digs out an unbridgeable gulf between them. No, she never reaches out to her male readers. The female ones, sometimes, when she senses that they have experienced the fault line that undermines any hope of understanding, that they know the limitations of a relationship that they got into so simply. But the male ones, never: she flees them like a memory of pain or the certitude of failure, like men's vanity or the fear of being alone, alone among them, alone with them.

SHE NEVER TELLS men, the perfect strangers she wants to seduce as a stranger, that she writes. She isn't looking for readers, she'd prefer them to read her eyes.

The Student

THE STUDENT EXISTS only in the singular, he's a collective young man, a fluctuating collection. All students make up the student.

When she was twenty-two, the student was seventeen. Even if a century went by, he still would be. This is why the student must always have a definite article that designates him as something determined, familiar, and eternal: the student is like the *Mona Lisa*— a painting in a museum, a bust in a collection of sculptures, a statue. She remembers a nude Hermes in the Louvre who, before being protected by a surrounding rope, had been touched, stroked, and caressed so often that this stone penis was worn down, polished, almost flat; he now offers just two attributes to desire: either you regret not being able to reach out and touch that body, as others were able to do before you, or else you accept that, even if he is a spatial contemporary, there, fully formed before your eyes, he is also from a different time, eternal, beautiful, untouchable.

When the student writes or reads, bent over some immensity, she looks at him and rediscovers that delicious pleasure—a visit to the museum. She observes him from behind, his back, his shoulders, his nape, in springtime his arms below his short or rolled-up sleeves, the way his hand moves toward his temple or neck. Sometimes, he looks at her, their eyes meet, and she sees where the painter has concentrated his genius—it was so long ago, but the body is a living one, and its smile is delightful.

For the student, she has a sort of sublime love that arises at once from beauty and from that piercing sensation of the vanity of desire; she doesn't reach out to touch this mystery; what's more, the work sometimes comes to life, words cross those fleshy lips and their clichéd absurdity or whining tone freeze the hand of love just as surely as the *Mona Lisa*'s moustache draws a line over our hidden dreams.

The First Love

SHE CALLS HIM one Sunday morning—she's at home, alone, sad, it's one of those days when the past glitters like buried treasure and the phone book is the map. He hasn't moved, simply multiplied his means of communication—fax, e-mail—he's easy to get hold of, to get back hold of.

The phone rings for a long time, it's nearly twelve, she imagines that he's gone away for the weekend, where, who with, she knows nothing about him anymore, she regrets not hearing his voice, but oddly enough he doesn't have an answering machine. At that precise moment he answers, she doesn't recognize his husky voice, his slightly bored drawl, but it's him all right. "Were you asleep?" she asks after saying her name, "were you asleep?" as if it wasn't years ago that she rushed down his staircase never to appear again in his life except in photographs, are you asleep, my first love, do you still sleep at the same incredible depth, apparently you do, that's right, you slept through thunderstorms, nothing could wake you, I remember that, except for a finger stroking the curve of your eyebrows. "Oh, it's you!" he mutters with an unfriendly sigh, "but it is twelve o'clock," she says, not so much to excuse this intrusion (maybe he isn't alone, maybe he took a girl back home with him last night) as to give a logical justification for her call:

with astonishment, she hears herself pronounce those reproach-
ful words, "but it is twelve o'clock," as if she was on time for
some date fixed long ago and he wasn't, because he was careless,
slovenly, dishonest, forgetful, and—no, she suddenly tells herself
(she ought to hang up), it's more as if, while dashing down those
stairs all those years ago, I tried to alleviate his disappointment, to
conceal my flight, by making this vague arrangement from the bot-
tom of the steps: "I'll call you tomorrow at twelve"—and maybe
she did so, that day, she can't remember now, perhaps she'd really
said "Speak to you tomorrow at twelve," and ten years later she
calls, hello it's me, it's twelve o'clock.

FIRST LOVE IS eternal, time doesn't pass by, that's the principle
of first love. History is not shaped like a row of moving carriages
drawing ever farther away from the platform and its waving hand-
kerchiefs, it is more like an old fairy tale in which you can find the
sleeping loved one, the lover, without even having to cross a dark
wood, he would be there waiting, his face full of trust in both of
you, his arms relaxed in the abandon of sleep, he'd wake up when
you touched him, kissed him, this prince with his unchanging
charm, that patient angel for whom a hundred years is nothing,
"it's you," he'd say on opening his eyes, you've been a long time
coming, it's true, but he'd love you as he did that first day with the
timeless love of children's dreams.

The Stranger

WHAT SHE EXPECTS from the stranger is both much and little. She expects him to discover and reveal her as if he were an explorer sent to some unknown land; to name and accept her in the time they share together, as a man does with his children; to be tender and generous, as if she had saved his life. To the stranger, she is shiftless, nameless, and fearless; she has neither ties nor laws; to the stranger, she's also his stranger. Yet, as soon as he draws near, he acquires more knowledge than anyone else; by making love he knows her because he recognizes her—it's her, that woman in his arms who remembers him as though recalling a forgotten word. The stranger knows nothing about her, but he knows who she is, he confirms her identity and reassures her very self. She has no knowledge about the stranger, but she knows him, all right, she knows him like the back of her hand.

IN SEX with strangers, she looks for and finds this mutual feeling that, in time, is often called *love* and that, at moments when bodies are touched by emotions they both feel and cause, she, as though saying "thanks" or "hello" or "it's you," simply calls *recognition*.

Alone with Him

I have a dubious morality, you know, *I find others' morality dubious.*

Fidelity is an empty word, blind vanity, as if you possessed something, as if you thought you were immortal, as if you really were.

The fact of the matter is that I've started loving men the way I love my children—my daughters: when I hold them in my arms, ever since they were tiny, ever since they were babies, I've always known that their warmth will abandon me one day, that those bodies I caress with all my love will leave me, I know they'll go and I won't even know where to find them, since the beginning I've sensed that absence in the crook of the sweetest arms, the solitude the other leaves you in, even if he loves you, in which he finally leaves all of us, even if he comes back, the solitude that is also his, his irreducible difference.

That's also what gives me pleasure in love, in all the forms of love: what pleasures me is physical presence, I love the present and the body. That's right, men are like big kids. They leave, I can't stop them. They have their liberty, so they take liberties, there's no love, only tokens of love, don't you agree? The body is the sole token of love—or rather, no, not the only one: free men can leave, and sometimes they stay—that's the finest token of love, to take the liberty of staying when you could go.

I think this comparison between men and children is a good one. Do we demand the fidelity we expect from husbands and lovers—a monogamy of the flesh because they've been inside us, in our bellies—from our sons and daughters, do we ask a child to remain faithful to its mother because it's lived inside her, do we demand from it that eternally stupid, vain recognition—recognition of having been in our bellies? Go on, go away, I know you love me—why should I add ties of flesh and blood to the thousand chains that already bind us together?

The Husband

SHE LOVES to watch the husband playing with the children, the girls, "well, girls, what shall we do?" he says. She watches them take over the father's body, assail him, clamber up his back, grab his neck, run screaming into his arms. The father lets them, he puts up with everything, they pull his moustache, jump on his stomach, pummel him—the father is a conquered land.

Whenever she looks at her daughters, she loves her husband. She loves the similarities between them and him, even their faults, she likes everything about them. She understands why people stay together "for the children," she can understand this perfectly, it seems to her to be an excellent reason. She never wearies of the eternal surprise, the miracle made possible by a man: girls with dark blue eyes. Making love, making babies, isn't this justification enough for the bonds of wedlock and for keeping them tied? Shouldn't we, above all else, be eternally thankful to the man who gave us what is, after all, a gift, whatever people say, a gift of himself, can we forget what he has given, what he was good enough to give, would that be fair?

She doesn't find the old expression "father of my children" at all stupid, she even thinks it's the best description of the bond between them, how, even though she no longer loves him, she still does. The husband may no longer be the love of her life. But when she sees him topple down onto the rug, besieged, when she contemplates their three bodies as they run toward the sea screaming, the girls swimming and taking breaths as he's taught them to do, those pure gestures, their hearts beating, she still loves him, she loves him for always, because he's the father of her daughters, because, in the strictest sense of the term, he is the love of her life.

The Father

WHEN HE'S SIXTY, someone offers to buy the father's practice. He hasn't reached retirement age yet, but he agrees—he's had enough of stumps, the noise of the drill, and garlic breath. He lives alone in a two-room flat, he'll be able to get by until his pension starts.

When he's sixty, something suddenly cracks open in the father's life. It looks as if he's becoming happy.

He signs up for all sorts of courses, goes rafting, hang gliding, flying, snowmobiling, bungee jumping, canyoning, and mono-skiing. She sometimes wonders if he's gone crazy, if he's trying to kill himself. She remembers her grandfather, who carried on smoking heavily after having several strokes. She no longer knows the truth about men: do they not fear death, or do think they're immortal?

THE FATHER TAKES flying lessons at the aerodrome, goes gliding, takes pilot manuals home with him, and gets his license. From then on, he spends every day out there, flying when the weather's good or repairing fuselage in icy hangars during the winter. He's the club's unpaid secretary, an in-house mechanic, a giver of maiden flights, and he camps out on Pic Saint-Loup with a group of teenagers, where he tells them saucy Jean Rigaud stories amid peels of laughter.

When he's sixty-five, he takes up aerobatics and learns how to loop the loop and do nosedives. It's all he talks about—the heady feeling in the sky, the freedom, the joy of flying—*all my life I dreamed.*

ONE DAY, he comes to see her at her place, the girls are at the swimming pool with their father, they sit in the garden where for the last hour he's been describing his latest session at Saint-Crépin and the sensation of flying so close to the mountains. She interrupts him to ask when that was—last weekend?

"No," he says. "I didn't go flying last weekend. I went to my mother's funeral."

She tries to hold back a sentence that is out of control, her face is like a clown's white mask, she says:

"Oh, really! Is your mother dead then?"

HE WENT TO the funeral, he hesitated for some time before going, but in the end he went. There, he saw his half-brothers and -sisters, that's right, his mother had other children afterward, with . . .

"What about him?" she can't resist asking (she never asks her father anything, this is a golden opportunity, otherwise she'll never know). "Him, I mean, her, I mean the father of her . . ." (him, yes, him, the one his mother abandoned everything for, who was he, what sort of man was he, what sort of man does a mother leave for?) "Was he there?"

"Him? No. He must be already dead. She was eighty-five."

"But what did he do, for a living that is, I mean, do you know how they met?"

"No, I don't. He was a businessman, I think, at least that's what my mother told me when she came to the house—you remember, I suppose—over twenty-five years ago! But I'm not sure now, and I never saw him."

HE FALLS SILENT for a long time, he closes up, then, suddenly, as if a memory has come back to him to his own amazement, he points a forefinger at her, as she hides her crimson cheeks behind her teacup, and says:

"No, all I can remember about him is his hobby, a passion he'd had ever since he was young—he was a real red devil, that's how my mother put it—his passion was airplanes. He was a pilot."

Alone with Him

DO YOU REALLY believe that? Do you really think I'm coming here for "marriage counseling" all on my own, twice a week, regular as clockwork, in an attempt to patch things up, to prop up the ruins?

I come here because I have an appointment—I'm here to make appointments, because I need you. I come because I have an appointment with you and without you I'd only have disappointments, that's why.

Of course, you will say—I can just hear you, it's as if I can hear you—you will say: it isn't me, I'm not the one she's speaking to, I'm not the one she's looking at; it's a transfer, the staging of the Other, oh yes, I know a little about that.

It must be terrible never to be loved for what you are, always to be the Other, and never Yourself. It must be awful to make that your profession.

But I am talking to you and I am looking at you. I'm no Taoist grand master, I don't refrain from choice. I know what I'm doing, I know that I'm looking at you. It's you, it can only be you.

The Father

SHORTLY AFTER his mother's funeral, the father calls her—he
has something to tell her: he's going to get married.

She doesn't ask, as he once did, "who against?" She doesn't say
that coincidentally she is going to get divorced. She senses that
nothing should be taken away from the joyous gravity of this moment, that what she should do is consider her father to be like a son
about to leave home to fend for himself. What's more, didn't he
say "I'm going to get married" and not "get married again"? No,
you can't start all over at almost seventy, but you can quite simply
start.

She remembers how, when they were children, she and her sister used to hide under the dining room table in the hope of sneak-
ing a glimpse of what the father hid beneath the towel he tied around
his hips when he emerged from the shower. They never managed
to see a thing—maybe there was nothing there, maybe when it was
of no further use it was cut off, some religions insist on that, so
maybe Protestants did, too—they just didn't know.

It was a mystery that haunted them for a long time, because of
the expression he sometimes used with a breeziness that deepened
the mystery: "You were still in your dad's bollocks."

She'd tried to picture this past, which preceded her birth, which was prior to her mother's womb, a virile enclosure in which she and her father were united—in a male origin. She'd never succeeded, of course, her sister was presumably right, they did cut off the family jewels when they were of no further use: the third daughter had died at birth, so she was the last living being to have inhabited the father's sexual organs in a way that could make love last and incarnate it. Of course, she wasn't exactly alone, there was also Claude—not the only one, but the last one, isn't it something to be the father's last love? Well, no, in fact she's neither the only one nor the last one. This one is fifty, has three children, all her own teeth—she's a dental nurse, it was in fact in his very own surgery that he met her thirty years before, she was doing a six-month training course, she was already in love with him back then, that's for sure, but at the time nothing was possible (nothing, love). A complete coincidence brought them back together again, he ran into her in a café, he recognized her, and here we are—they're getting married next week.

SO IT'S LATE in life that she learns what her father has always had hidden beneath his towel: it's nothing like the precious jewels that she thought were men's most jealously kept secret, but a dream pinned to their bodies, a fixed passion that she thought her mother alone was racked by and that she must now, whatever the cost, keep up as her double inheritance: to love, and be loved.

The Husband

SOMETHING'S UP with the husband. He doesn't raise his head when she comes in, he looks out the window at a steady stream of almost Norman rain, he gazes at the garden with the blue determination of a Viking contemplating his own shipwreck, "a leak in the drake," she says to herself as she takes off her coat, but she's wrong, it's no leak, it's a gaping hole.

His mistress of the past few months is pregnant. No, she wasn't on the pill, she thought she was sterile—chronic endometriosis, blocked Fallopian tubes, well anyway, now look.

"What about you?" she says, sitting down in front of him— she sees his barbarian profile, his cheek where a tense nerve is beating, while the other side of his face, in the window, is drowning in tears.

"I really do not want her to have the child, I mean, really not, you believe me, don't you?"

"What about her?"

The husband says nothing, and in that stretch of silence, a child takes shape, she can see it, she feels gripped by a sort of jollity, she can see it in his arms, as if it was already there. Ten years before, her jaw would have frozen and her fists clenched with fury; now it's all as familiar as saying hello, things are as simple as life or death: a blueprint with distinct marks, clear lines tracing out a world in which men have babies with women and mortals strive to ward off death.

"She's going to have an abortion."

He doesn't want it, so there's an end to it, what would he do with another one, anyway, and why have one, after all, why? OK, so he makes love with her, fine, great, he found her attractive, he wanted her, he got her, he's happy—she's a lovely girl, in fact, he really likes her a lot, but that's as far as it goes. Period.

And she's surely the last person in the world who's going to talk him into it?

She doesn't know—she mumbles out some platitude, something like "you have to take things as they come" or "that's life" or "think it over."

"Life! What are you talking about? This, is life?"

And he starts speaking. And it seems to her that his words are tumbling into an abyss.

WHAT HE LIKES about women is the distance they create between them and him, so that he must cross it. He's a player, he takes a chance, he's a hunter, he wants to overcome. Then (as she well knows) there is pleasure, the forgetting of yourself in another, for a moment. But he has nothing else to offer—nothing at all, he's thought it over carefully.

She remembers his arms around her waist that first night when, after making long slow love, they smooched together as the party ended, among the empty glasses, the full ashtrays, and the smell of exhausted bodies. She was floating, borne up by her trust in him, dumb, blind, and deaf to everything but the beating of their hearts.

Life—life? She's completely off the track, she obviously can't understand a thing: life doesn't concern him for the simple reason that he's dead. Leaving aside courtship rituals, everything else for him dissolves into disgust, denial, horror: for example, he detests rotting flesh, he can't stop thinking about all the intestines, guts, and shit in a body.

"They're very nice with their love, but what happens when I want to take a shit, where am I supposed to go? Then all I can think about is running away, vanishing before the smell starts up, the gases, the stink, the foul breath, everyone has to hide to relieve himself of his misery, and they hug me in their arms, 'don't go, stay a little longer'—and I should already be out of there, I should have left them in my magnificence, in perfect agreement, before things topple down again, before I croak, because we all do croak, didn't you realize that? And a child now, is it? That really would be insane, I can't father a child now, it's already an uphill struggle with the ones I've got, no, not any more, I don't have enough life left, enough faith—even if you, even if you yourself asked me to. All I can do is fuck, and then only if they shut up, then it's OK, I can still carry off the illusion, make believe, make love as though I was still alive. But it's fake, as fake as you can get—I can tell you all this because you understand everything (just don't repeat it): I'm a dead man who comes."

Alone with Him

SO I THOUGHT, I didn't say it, but I thought: I'd rather have a living man who loves.

MEN ARE ALWAYS more wrapped up in death. What crime have they committed to make them seek atonement in oblivion? Is it a country, a homeland, where they feel that they will leave their bodies one day, and lose themselves more thoroughly than in violence or love?

André

EARLY ONE MORNING, her mother phones. André died during the night, he cried out, she put on the light, he was dead. She can't stay alone with the body, she just can't, it's André's body.

She takes the first train, it's raining, it's snowing, she crosses all of France. Her thoughts go to the dead in her life that she has seen—her baby, her grandmother. Not a single man—she didn't go back into her grandfather's room after the evening of poetry, she has kept a memory of the smell of tobacco and three days' growth, which made him look like an adventurer used to the dangers of travel who was carrying on regardless; she remembers being told later that he had been in agony because of chronic priapism and that he'd showed his huge swollen member to the nurse asking her, if she so desired, to take advantage of what death still had to offer, while his wife was talking to the priest and trying to convince him that he'd misheard and that the old boy hadn't called him a ball-less wonder.

The countryside passes before her eyes, orchards, vineyards, meadows, towns, power plants whose smoke at dusk looks like the cremation of the world, the stations where the living meet and part. Then she remembers, she has seen a dead man, of course she has, she saw him so often how on earth could she have forgotten:

her husband, dead, stretched out on a hospital trolley, like the ones
you see in morgues, his silent motionless love, his features frozen
into sadness, a hint of rancor perhaps, but how to tell when his
eyes are closed? During the early years, she saw him a hundred
times, killed, dead, and gone, every time he was five minutes late
she said good-bye forever, it was all over, never again would he
hold her in his arms, he'd faded into the landscape along with one
of his sports cars, she started to cry, and when he was resurrected
at the end of the corridor, holding his keys, she'd rush over to him,
come on, take me in your arms, was that the secret of love, then: a
body where you can rest your cheek, a body with a beating heart?

ANDRÉ IS DRESSED in a beautiful blue herringbone suit, they
had been spoiled for choice in his splendid wardrobe. She's touched
by men's elegance, she feels that, rather than being a symptom of
vanity, it reveals a certain courtesy toward women, an appreciable
desire to please those who try to please them. She sits down beside
him, on the edge of the bed, in a familiar way, and holds his hand
for a long time, as you would with a sick lover, she can't take her
eyes off him—it's him, André, it's really him—never before has
she looked at a man for so long.

Later, the next day, she rummages through a large box of
photographs. She sees André again, as he was when, as a child, she
used to gaze at him: dark hair, blue eyes, ivory cigarette holder. On
the front of a box of matches, she discovers the two of them, him
and her mother, cheek to cheek, smiling at the camera like stars at
the Cannes Film Festival, on the back there's the name of a nightclub in Juan-les-Pins—this is no longer *Au Théâtre Ce Soir*, it's
more like *La Dolce Vita*. As for the mischievous little girl, living
out her life alongside them in other shots, in other locations, she
can see herself in the photographer's eye already testing out her
ability to be loved, to make others love her, as if there was any-

thing you can do to be loved. She'd like to take the box of matches, but she doesn't dare. She returns to André, sits back down again, contemplates him again, cries over days long gone while her mother is arguing on the phone—will she still receive his pension, what forms must she fill in, and has the embalmer made out his bill yet, she might not be able to settle it straightaway, would they mind waiting till the bank . . . and, yes, of course, if there's no alternative they can take him out through the window, if the body really won't go around the bend in the stairs, then the window will have to do, just so long as they don't trample on the rosebushes. She squeezes his stiff pockmarked hand: "Well, well, André, once a Romeo, always a Romeo, a lover till you got married, and now you're escaping through the window."

THEY STAY THERE for three days. She's outside of time, she has no more husband, children, work, or future. She looks at André, dead.

A silent communing. Death has no hold on her. No, what scares her in this moment of suspension, in which the past is shifting like a slow waltz (roses, kisses, champagne, the wait behind the curtains), is that love—men's love—comes to an end.

Alone with Him

IN THE END, how do you know when it's over, how can you tell when it's done—the book, the analysis, love?

I won't be coming back, this is the last appointment. There we are, I sit down, I look at you, I break the agreement, it's over.

There's a man in my eyes—do you see him from where you're sitting, can you see him? Come nearer, come on, you can't see a thing from where you are, you're too far away.

Is it finished for you, or is it beginning? That's for you to say— I won't be coming back, I've finished my book, or nearly, but I'd like to begin with you, a new start in life, a love story. So is it finished for you?

YOU'RE TOO FAR AWAY.

How do you know when it's over—do I love my husband, do I love you—what do I know?

If I'm nuts, what do you know about it?

COME ON, come here, please join me, don't stay over there, let's not leave it there, make an effort, don't leave me to do everything, move, make a sign, do it for me.

I'm here. Look at me.

Do you want me to get on my knees and beg?

Take me in your arms.

YOU'RE STAYING far away, where you are? But what are you without me? The woman is the body of the man, the man is the body of the woman. We are, one to the other, what keeps us alive.

Come on, I miss you, I'm missing you, without you, everything's missing, you are the only thing that protects me from the dead.

Come nearer, I beg of you, your body. All I want is a body, a wordless body, an ordinary body.

Come on, we're so close. Now it's up to you to be me, and me to be you—a single body made of our two single bodies. You're alone. Did you know that?

I'm not sure anymore. Are you the same? Are you different? Do you love me? Are you indifferent?

I love you. Do you feel concerned?

The Editor

THE EDITOR PHONES one Sunday. He wants to know if he'll soon get to see the final chapters of the novel that is still unfinished for some unknown reason, which, to judge by the tone of his voice, he has guessed. He doesn't twist her arm by insisting on dates and deadlines, he just says that he's dying to read those words that have been promised for so long.

She's touched by the fact that he's phoning on a Sunday—like the first time—it may be a coincidence, maybe not. She tells him that it's finished, that now all they have to do is name it, find a definitive title. She would also like to include at some point, it doesn't really matter where, the following disclaimer: "This book is a novel. All its men are fictitious." She leaves him to decide, but it is important to her.

She likes his voice as it garners information, questioning, impatient—a voice that wants to know. She likes the way he shows his enthusiasm openly, with a sort of *anticipatory delight* that suddenly seems to her to be a sign of great love.

And an image arises, filling her mind with its terrifying banality and vivid truth, an image she cannot possibly have seen, but that she pictures now: the father pacing up and down the corridor, a cigarette in his mouth, worried, happy though he doesn't yet know what about, who about, happy about what he's expecting, what's coming, happy about what's on the way; the anxious, fretful father, for whom she would be both daughter and wife, newborn babe and beloved woman, the expected one and the pleasurable one, the one you hope for and the one you cherish—the desired voice and body: the event, the happy event, advent; the father with his gleam of hope and, at the same time, given the greatness of his expectations, the looming threat of disappointment; the father who's no longer expectant, who knows what it is: it's her.

TO ANSWER DESIRE, to satisfy expectations, to be an object for all their hopes: a little girl, a woman, a book—an object of love.

Abel Waits

SHE WON'T BE back. She tells him: come what may, this is the last time. She pays for the consultation, she places two banknotes on the desk and, above them, in full view, an invitation to *La Traviata* the next evening.

SHE'S SITTING with her program on her lap, staring in a dream fixedly at the heavy blue velvet curtain, as if it were the deep blue sea. The opera house resonates with the rumor of a thousand muffled conversations, people are telling one another their life stories, she thinks, you spend your life doing that.

He arrives at the very moment that the houselights dim and silence falls—did he hesitate before coming, did he want to avoid meeting her eyes, avoid speaking? She doesn't look around, she knows it's him—*fors'è lui*.

SHE'S LYING on the sofa in his place and reading an article he's just written for a learned journal—did she inspire it? "Love is powerless, even when reciprocated, because it does not know that it is merely the desire to be One, and this makes it impossible to establish a dual relationship. What results is neither unified nor dual, but a *gender duel.*" And it concludes with the following Lacan quote: "There is no love, only tokens of love." She wonders if she's understood what should be understood, and if the meaning is the same as in the dreary dialogues of the dreary novels she used to devour:

"Do you love me?"

"Yes."

"Then give me a token of your love."

He's sitting at his desk, she can see him from behind as he types something into his computer—he's recently got interested in the new economy.

"Next month," she says, "there's a James Bowman recital. We could go together, it's on a Saturday evening when I won't have the girls and you won't have the boys." (She adores countertenors— that male voice coming from a man's body in which a woman is singing.)

"Next month? Well, if you insist."

He begins his sentence while staring at the columns of figures parading across his screen, then he turns around to look at her— and, like every time, his stare grips her with a darting sensation— he reminds her of someone, his face rings a bell; she has, there sitting in front of her, her own nostalgia for him—he turns around and, arm laid on the back of the chair, says:

"Because, well, to be perfectly frank, ever since I was a child, I've always detested music."

The Recipient

THE RECIPIENT RECEIVES what he is given. He says nothing, he doesn't answer back. The recipient isn't a correspondent, for him, reception is a one-way process, he must remain in the shadow of the silence where we know he is listening. The recipient's acceptance of his discreet destiny is vital, you must never doubt it, never, you must be sure of it.

I'M WRITING for you, I'm writing you. I know that women are the real readers but I'd be incapable of writing if I didn't think, even in the vaguest way, as a shape against the light, that you are a man. You're the one I'm talking to, I'm talking about you, about you and me. I don't know who you are, but I can see you, I intuit you, I paint you, I recount you, I invent you: I write you.

WHO ARE YOU? I don't know. I have no idea who you are.

AND PLEASE DON'T reply. There's no point. We can't correspond with each other, there's no possible correspondence between us. You're distant, you're Other, you're man. I've accepted this distance that fluctuates between us like the path of a letter as it travels. I'm not expecting you to answer and yet I am still writing you. Don't let that surprise you: I may have given up trying to grasp you, but not the motion of grasping you. Writing is that motion, I'm writing toward you. It's like the waving hand when the train has gone: useless, but not pointless.

I USED TO expect an answer, I suppose, that you would tell me, explain to me. I questioned the men of books, poets, characters, I imagined that one day life would flow beneath the bridge of our arms. And then I read that story that devotes the world to writing: the one about the little boy who wants his mother to kiss him before he goes to bed and all he receives in answer to his declaration of love are these few words of loneliness: "There is no answer."

When this sense was given to me, it freed me from so much absence, so many expectations. Thus, I don't write for you to answer; I write because there is no answer. Never will I be held in your arms—nor you in mine—never will we kiss.

YET SOMETIMES, I dream of how to get us together. Often, when asleep—Morpheus rocks me and I glimpse how to draw out that loving sleep whose god is a man. Then I see you—you're on the brink of oblivion, but I can still see you, you reach out your arms toward me and I come to you, I go to you, my destined one— my recipient. Who said you were a woman? How absurd! Death take your eyes, but it's still on your chest that I'll lay my head, I know that, on your shoulders that I'll place my hands. It's you, it's really you on the distant shore, the space between us is dwindling, soon it will be gone, come on, let's dance, I'm with you and you embrace me—take me, take me, I'm gone—oh ain't it nice, yes, ain't it nice in those arms!

ABOUT THE AUTHOR

Born in Dijon, France, CAMILLE LAURENS is the author of six previous novels and two works of nonfiction. *In His Arms,* winner of the Prix Femina, was a number one best-seller in France and is Laurens's first book to be translated into English. A librarian, she lives in France.

ABOUT THE TYPE

This book is set in Fournier, a typeface named for Pierre Simon Fournier, the youngest son of a French printing family. Pierre Simon first studied watercolor painting, but became involved in type design through work that he did for his eldest brother. Starting with engraving woodblocks and large capitals, he later moved on to fonts of type. In 1736 he began his own foundry and published the first version of his point system the following year. He made several important contributions in the field of type design; he cut and founded all the types himself, pioneered the concepts of the type family, and is said to have cut sixty thousand punches for 147 alphabets of his own design. He also created new printers' ornaments.

Pierre Simon Fournier is probably best remembered as the designer of St. Augustine Ordinaire, one of the early transitional faces. It served as the model for the Monotype transitional face, Fournier, which was released in 1925.